She might not be the jezebel he thought she was, but women like Lily Wild always knew what they were about.

He'd had enough of the simmering tension between them and knew just how to kill it dead.

"Okay, that's it," he said softly, placing his empty glass on the antique sideboard with deliberate care. "I'm giving you fair warning. I'm sick of the tension between us and the reason for it. You've got exactly three seconds to get moving before I take up from what we started six years ago, but this time there'll be no stopping. You're not seventeen anymore and there's no secretary to interrupt like yesterday. This time we're on our own and I'm not in the mind to stop at one kiss, and neither, I suspect, are you."

Scandal in the Spotlight

The truth is more shocking than the headline!

Named and most definitely shamed, these media darlings have learned the hard way that the press always loves a scandal!

Having devastatingly gorgeous men on their arms only adds fuel to the media frenzy. Especially when the attraction between them burns hotter and brighter than a paparazzo's flash bulb...

Look for more Scandals in the Spotlight, coming soon!

Michelle Conder

GIRL BEHIND THE SCANDALOUS REPUTATION

TORONTO NEW YORK LONDON
AMSTERDAM PARIS SYDNEY HAMBURG
STOCKHOLM ATHENS TOKYO MILAN MADRID
PRAGUE WARSAW BUDAPEST AUCKLAND

Recycling programs
for this product may
not exist in your area.

ISBN-13: 978-0-373-23834-7

GIRL BEHIND THE SCANDALOUS REPUTATION

Copyright © 2012 by Michelle Conder

All about the author...
Michelle Conder

From as far back as she can remember **MICHELLE CONDER** dreamed of being a writer. She penned the first chapter of a romance novel just out of high school, but it took much study, many (varied) jobs, one ultra-understanding husband and three very patient children before she finally sat down to turn that dream into a reality.

Michelle lives in Australia, and when she isn't busy plotting she loves to read, ride horses, travel and practice yoga.

This is Michelle Conder's first novel for Harlequin Presents® and we hope you love it as much as we do!

For Paul, who always takes the kids—even when it means missing a surf, for my kids, who so graciously accept when Mummy is busy,
for Laurel, who tirelessly
reads my dodgy first drafts, and for Mum, who is always there when I need her most. And for Flo for her keen insights and endless encouragement.
Thank you all.

CHAPTER ONE

'Is this your idea of a joke, Jordana?' Tristan Garrett turned away from the view of the Thames outside his tenth-storey office window to stare incredulously at his baby sister. She sat in one of the navy tub chairs on the visitors' side of his desk, legs crossed, immaculately groomed, and looking not at all like a crazy person sailing three sheets to the wind—as she sounded.

'As if I would joke about something so serious!' Jordana exclaimed, gazing at him, her jade-green eyes, the exact shade of his own, wide and etched with worry. 'I know it sounds unbelievable but it's true, and we have to help her.'

Actually, her story didn't sound unbelievable at all, but Tristan knew his sanguine sister had a tendency to see goodness in people when there was none to see at all.

He turned back to stare at the pedestrians lining the Thames and better able to enjoy the September sunshine than he was. He couldn't stand seeing his sister so upset, and he cursed the so-called friend who was responsible for putting these fresh tears in her eyes.

When she came to stand beside him he slung his arm around her shoulders, drawing her close. What could he say to placate her? That the friend she wanted to help wasn't worth it? That anyone stupid enough to try and smuggle drugs out of Thailand deserved to get caught?

Normally he would help his sister in a heartbeat, but no way was he getting involved in this fiasco—and nor was she. He gave her an affectionate squeeze, but he didn't try to contain the edge of steel in his voice when he spoke. 'Jo, this is not your problem and you are not getting involved.'

'I—'

Tristan held up his hand to cut off her immediate objection, his solid-gold cufflinks glinting in the downlights. 'If what you say is true then the girl made her bed and she'll have to lie in it. And may I remind you that you're eight days away from the wedding of the year. Not only will Oliver not want you getting involved, but I doubt the Prince of Greece will want to sit beside a known drug-user—no matter how beautiful.'

Jordana's mouth tightened. 'Oliver will want me to do what's right,' she objected. 'And I don't care what my wedding guests think. I'm going to help Lily and that's that.'

Tristan shook his head. 'Why would you risk it?'

'She's my best friend and I promised I would.'

That surprised him. He'd thought their friendship had died down years ago. But if that was the case then why was Lily to be maid of honour at Jo's wedding? Maid of honour to *his* best man! And why hadn't he thought to ask that question two weeks earlier, when he'd found out Lily was coming to the wedding?

He frowned, but decided to push that issue aside for the more pressing problem at hand. 'When did you speak to her?'

'I didn't. A customs officer called on her behalf. Lily wanted to let me know why she couldn't meet me, and— Oh, Tristan, if we don't help her she'll probably go to jail.'

Tristan pushed back the thick lock of hair that had fallen over his forehead and made a mental note to book a haircut.

Much as he didn't want to, he could see that he needed to get tough with his sister. 'Which is probably the best place for her.' He scowled. 'She'll be able to get help there.'

'You don't mean that!'

Didn't he? He didn't know. But what he did know was that his morning had been a lot better before Jordana had rushed into his office, bringing to mind a girl he'd rather strip from it altogether.

Honey Blossom Lily Wild.

Currently voted one of the sexiest women on the planet, and a talented actress to boot. He didn't follow films but he'd seen her first one—some art-house twaddle made by a precocious upstart of a director about the end of the world. Tristan couldn't remember the plot. What man could? It had Lily naked, save for a white oversized singlet and a pair of cotton panties masquerading as shorts, in almost every scene. The movie had signified to him that as a culture they were heading backwards—and people like Lily Wild were half the reason for that.

He and his father had tolerated the girls' teenage friendship because it had made Jordana happy—and neither man would ever have jeopardised that—but Tristan had disliked Lily on sight when he'd first come across her as a gangly fourteen-year-old, hiding drugs under his sister's dormitory mattress. She'd been haughty beyond her years that day, and if he had his time again he'd suggest his sister be relocated to another boarding school quick-smart.

Tristan heaved a sigh and returned to the smooth curve of his walnut desk, stroking his computer mouse to get rid of the screen saver. 'Jo, I'm busy. I have an important meeting in half an hour. I'm sorry, but I can't help.'

'Tristan, I know you have a thing about drug-users, but Lily is innocent.'

'And you know this how, exactly?' he queried, deciding that humouring his sister might expedite her leaving.

'Because I know Lily, and I know she doesn't take drugs. She hates them.'

Tristan raised an eyebrow. Was his sister for real? 'Have you conveniently forgotten the fallout from your eighteenth birthday party? How I caught her hiding a joint when she was fourteen? Not to mention the various press photos of her completely wasted in between.'

Jordana frowned and shook her head. 'Most of those photos were fakes. Lily's been hounded by the press her whole life because of who her parents were—and, anyway, she's far too sensible and level-headed to get involved in something as destructive as drugs.'

'And that would be why there was the scandal at your eighteenth? Because Lily is *so* level-headed?'

Jordana glanced at the ceiling before returning resigned eyes to his. 'Tristan, that night was so not what it seemed. One dodgy photo—'

'One dodgy photo?' he all but shouted. 'One dodgy photo that could have destroyed your reputation if I hadn't intervened!'

'You mean if you hadn't made Lily take the blame!'

'Lily *was* to blame!' Tristan could feel the old anger of six years ago welling up inside him. But it wasn't like him to let his temper override common sense and he controlled it with effort. 'Maybe if I had contacted her stepfather when I caught her with marijuana the first time she wouldn't be in the colossal mess she is now.'

Jordana briefly lowered her eyes before meeting his again. 'Tristan, you've never let me properly explain about any of this. What if the marijuana you found Lily hiding when we were fourteen wasn't hers? Would you be so disappointed if it was mine?'

Tristan expelled a breath. He really didn't have time for this. He got up and rounded his desk to enfold Jordana in his arms. He knew what she was trying to do and he loved her for it—even if the little bimbo she was trying to protect didn't deserve her loyalty.

'I know you're trying to take the blame for her, Jo. You've always protected her. But the fact still remains that she's trouble. She always has been. Surely her stepfather or stepsisters can help her?'

Jordana sniffed against his chest and pushed away a little. 'They've never been very close, and anyway I think they're holidaying in France. Please, Tristan! The officer I spoke to this morning said she might be deported back to Thailand. And, no matter what you think, I can't let that happen.'

Tristan swore under his breath. He had to admit he didn't want to imagine the gorgeous Lily Wild wasting away in a Thai prison cell either. 'Jo, my specialty is corporate law, and this will fall under the criminal jurisdiction.'

'But surely you can do *something*!' she implored.

Tristan released his sister and stalked over to the floor-to-ceiling windows again.

Unwelcome images of Lily as he'd last seen her crowded in and he forcibly held them back. She had been intruding on his thoughts and dreams for years now, but more so of late. Ever since Jordana had mentioned she was coming to the wedding, in fact, and to say that he resented her for it was putting it mildly.

He closed his eyes, the better to control the physical reaction he always seemed to have when he pictured her, but that only made it worse. Now he could not only visualise her, he could almost scent her as well.

Jordana touched his arm, and for a split second he imagined it *was* Lily.

Tristan muttered another curse under his breath. 'Jo, forget Lily Wild and concentrate on your wedding,' he growled, feeling like a heel when his sister flinched back from him.

'If Lily's not going to be there I might not even *have* a wedding.'

'Now you're being melodramatic.'

'And you're being horrible. Lily's been unfairly targeted…'

'Jordana, the woman wasn't targeted. She was caught red-handed!'

Jordana looked at him with the kind of pain he hadn't seen in her eyes since the day they had buried their mother. He'd vowed then that he'd do anything to protect her in the future and safeguard her happiness, and wasn't what he was doing now the opposite?

But what she was asking was impossible…

'Tristan, I know you hate drugs because of Mum, but Lily isn't like that. And you usually jump at the chance to help a worthy cause.'

Tristan stared at Jordana. Her words brought back memories of the past he'd much rather leave dead and buried. And maybe it was somewhat illogical but he blamed Lily for that as well—because without her latest antics he wouldn't be having this conversation with his sister at all!

He turned back to face Jo and unclenched his jaw. 'Jordana, the key word in this situation is *worthy*. And as far as I'm concerned a drug-addicted actress who has hit the skids does not a worthy cause make.'

Jordana stared at him as if he'd just kicked a dog, and in that instant Tristan knew he was defeated. No way could he let his sister think so badly of him—and on top of that an image of Lily in a Thai prison cell kept swimming into his consciousness and twisting his gut.

He shook his head. 'This is a big mistake,' he warned, ignoring the little glow of relief he felt when Jordana's face lit up with unconcealed gratitude. 'And don't look at me like that. I might not be able to do anything. It's not like she shoplifted a bar of soap from the local chemist.'

'Oh, Tristan, you are the best brother in the world. Shall I wait and come with you?' Jordana was so happy she was practically singing.

Tristan looked up blankly, his mind already turning over to how he would approach the problem. When her words sank in his eyebrows shot skywards. 'Absolutely not.' The last thing he needed was his interfering sister getting in the way. 'I'll call you when

I know something. Now, go. Do wedding stuff, or something, and leave me to sort through this mess you're so determined to get us in the middle of.'

He barely registered it when she kissed his cheek and let herself out of his office, already issuing orders down the phone to his secretary. 'Kate, reschedule all my meetings for the afternoon and tell Stuart Macintyre I want him in my office five minutes ago.'

He eased back in his chair and blew out a breath.

Was he completely crazy to get involved with this?

Lily Wild was trouble, and if seeing her bent over his father's prized nineteenth-century Dickens desk snorting cocaine at Jo's eighteenth party wasn't proof enough of that, then surely her attempt to smuggle drugs through Heathrow today was.

Not that Lily had ever admitted to taking drugs the night of his sister's party. She'd just given him a phoney, imperious smile that had incited his temper to boiling and after that he hadn't wanted to hear any excuses. Why bother? In his experience all users were supposedly as innocent as Carmelite nuns.

And what had made him even more irate was that earlier that night Lily had looked at him with those violet-coloured doe eyes of hers as if he was the only man in the world for her. And, fool that he was, he'd very nearly bought it!

Up until that point she had been nothing more than an irritation, occasionally taking his sister to her stepfather's industry parties when they were too young, and running away from him whenever he had come across her at the family estate during school holidays.

But she hadn't run away from him at the party. Quite the opposite in fact.

Forget it, he told himself severely as his mind zeroed in on the potent memory of how he had danced with her that night. Touched her. Kissed her.

The realisation that he'd very nearly lost control with her still rankled. But she had tasted pure and sweet, and so hot and...

Tristan shook his head and swore violently. Instead of reliving a moment that should never have happened in the first place he should be remembering how he had come upon her in his father's private study with a group of social misfits, his beloved sister, and about half a kilo of cocaine.

It had taken ten minutes to have Security dispense with everyone but his sister, and twenty-four hours to shut down the internet photos of Jordana that had been taken on a guest's mobile phone.

The taste of Lily, unfortunately, had taken a little longer to shift.

Lily Wild squirmed uncomfortably on the hard metal chair she had been sitting in for the last four hours and seventeen minutes and wondered when this nightmare she was trapped in would end. She was presently alone in a small featureless room that would make any director on a cop show proud.

Earlier today she had been equal parts nervous and

excited at the prospect of returning to England, her home, for the first time in six years.

She had been lined up at border control for ages, and had just made it to the passport-check booth when the official behind the partition had directed her to a row of officers with sniffer dogs. She hadn't been concerned as she'd seen she was just one of many being checked over. Instead her mind had been on Jordana, hoping she would like the wedding present she'd bought for her and Oliver in Thailand, and also on how much she was looking forward to her long-overdue break.

Then one of the attending officers had lifted a medium-sized plastic bag out of her tote and asked if it belonged to her. She honestly hadn't been able to remember.

'I don't know,' she'd answered.

'Then you'll have to step this way.' He'd indicated a long, over-bright hallway and sweat had immediately prickled on her palms—like the heat rash she'd once developed while filming in Brazil.

Now, looking around the small featureless room, she wondered where the two customs officials had gone. Not that she missed them—particularly the smarmy younger one, who spoke almost exclusively to her chest and threatened to deport her to Thailand if she didn't start co-operating.

Which was a laugh in itself, because all she had done since they'd detained her was co-operate!

Yes, the multicoloured tote bag was hers. No, she

hadn't left it unattended at any time. Yes, a friend had been in her hotel room the night she'd packed. No, she didn't think he'd gone near her personal belongings. And doubly no, the small plastic vials filled with ecstasy and cocaine were not hers! She'd nearly had a heart attack at the question, sure they must have made a mistake.

'No mistake, ma'am,' the nicer of the two officials had said, and the prickle of sweat had made its way to her armpits and dripped down the back of her neck like a leaky tap.

They'd then questioned her for hours about her movements at Suvarnabhumi Airport and her reasons for being in Thailand until she was completely exhausted and couldn't remember what she'd told them. They'd left after that. No doubt to confer with those watching behind the two-way mirror.

Lily knew they suspected Jonah Loft, one of the guys working on the film she had just wrapped, but only because he had been in her room just before she had left for the airport. She felt terrible for him.

She had met Jonah at the New York rehabilitation centre she volunteered at, and it wouldn't take the authorities long to discover that he had once had a drug problem.

Fortunately he was over that now, but Lily knew from her work with addicts that if anything could set off a relapse it was people not believing in them. Which was why Lily had got him a job on the film in the first place. She had wanted to give him a second chance, but she supposed when they found out she had been the instigator of having him work on the film it would reflect badly on both of them.

And yet she knew he wouldn't have done this to her. He'd been too grateful—and hopeful of staying clean.

Lily sighed. Four hours and twenty-eight minutes.

Her bottom was numb and she stretched in the chair, wondering if she was allowed to get up and walk around. So far she hadn't, and her thigh muscles felt as if they had been petrified. She rubbed her temples to try and ease her aching head.

She hoped Jordana had been contacted so she wouldn't be concerned about why she hadn't made it through the arrival gate. Though, as to that, Jo would likely be more worried if she *did* know what was holding her up. Lily just prayed she didn't contact her overbearing brother for help.

The last thing she needed was the deliciously gorgeous but painfully autocratic Tristan Garrett finding out about her predicament. She knew he was supposed to be one of the best lawyers alive, but Lily had only ever had acrimonious dealings with Tristan—apart from ten unbelievably magic minutes on a dance floor at Jordana's eighteenth birthday party. Lily knew he hated the sight of her now.

He'd devastated her—first by kissing her in a way that had transported her to another world, and then by ignoring her for the rest of the night as if she hadn't even existed. As if they hadn't just kissed like soul mates…

And just when she'd thought her teenage heart couldn't break any more he'd come across her in his father's study trying to clean up a private party Jordana should never have been involved in, and jumped completely to the wrong conclusion.

He'd blamed Lily—and her 'kind'—and thrown her out of his home. In hindsight she supposed she should have been thankful that he'd taken the time to organise his chauffer to drive her the two hours back to London, but she hadn't been. She'd been crushed—and so had her stupid girlhood fantasy that he just might be the love of her life.

Looking back now, she couldn't imagine what had possessed her even to think that in the first place. They were from different worlds and she knew he had never approved of her. Had always been as disgusted as she was herself at her being the only offspring of two notoriously drugged-out hippy celebrities who had died—*in flagrante*—of a drug overdose.

Not that she'd ever let him see that. She did have some pride—not to mention her late father's wise words running through her head.

'Never let 'em know you care, Honeybee,' he'd always said. Of course he'd been referring mostly to rock music reviews, but she had never forgotten. And it had held her in good stead when she'd had to face down more than her fair share of speculation and scandal, thanks to her parents and, sometimes, to her own actions.

The hard scrape of the metal door snapped Lily back to the present and she glanced up as the smarmy customs official swaggered back into the room, a condescending smile expanding his fleshy lips.

He sat opposite her and cocked an eyebrow. 'You are one lucky lady, Miss Wild,' he said in his heavy cockney brogue. 'It seems you're to be released.'

Lily stared at him impassively, blinking against the harsh fluorescent light and giving nothing away as to how she was feeling.

The official sprawled back in the chair and rhythmically tapped the table with what looked like a typed report, staring at her chest. Men like him—men who thought that because she was blonde and had a nice face and reasonable body shape she was easy—were a dime a dozen.

This guy was a marine wannabe, with a flat-top haircut that, instead of adding an air of menace, made him look as if he should be in the circus. But even if he'd had the polish of some latter-day Prince Charming, Lily wouldn't have been interested. She might make movies about love and happy-ever-after but she wasn't interested in the fairy tale for herself. Not after her mother's experiences with Johnny Wild, and the humiliating sting of Tristan's rejection of her all those years ago.

'That's right,' Marine-man finally sneered when she remained silent. 'You celebrities always seem to know someone who knows someone, and then it's all peaches an' cream again. Personally, I would 'ave sent you back to Thailand to face the music. But lucky for you it ain't up to me.'

And thank heavens for that, Lily thought, trying not to react to his leering scrutiny.

'Sign these.' He shoved the stapled document across the table at her, all business for once.

'What is it?'

'Conditions of your release.'

Release? She really was being released? Heart thudding, and as if in slow motion, Lily took the sheets of paper, not daring to believe it was true. She bent forward, letting her long wavy hair swing forward to shield her face from his prying eyes. She was shaking so badly the words appeared blurry on the page.

When the door scraped open a second time she didn't bother to look up, assuming it was the other official, returning to oversee her signature. Then a prickly sensation raised the hairs on the back of her neck, and a deeply masculine and very annoyed voice shattered her concentration and stole the breath from her lungs.

'You'll find it's all in order, Honey, so just sign the damned release so we can get out of here.'

Lily squeezed her eyes shut and felt the throbbing in her head escalate. She'd recognise that chocolate-covered voice anywhere, and waited for the dots to clear behind her eyes before peering up to confirm that not only was her nightmare of a day not over, but it had just taken a distinct turn for the worst.

Fortunately Jordana had received the message about her delay, but unfortunately she'd done exactly what Lily had feared: she'd gone to her big brother for help.

CHAPTER TWO

LORD Garrett, Viscount Hadley, the future twelfth Duke of Greythorn, stood before her, with enough tension emanating from his body to fire a rocket to the moon.

'Tristan,' she breathed unnecessarily, her mind at once accepting that he was the most sublimely handsome male she had ever seen and rejecting that fact at the same time. He seemed taller and more powerful than she remembered, his lean, muscular physique highlighted by the precise cut of his tailor-made charcoal suit.

His chestnut hair was long, and lent him an untamed appeal he really didn't need, framing his olive complexion, flawlessly chiselled jaw and aristocratic nose to perfection. Her gaze skimmed up over the masculine curve of his lips and settled on cold, pale green eyes ringed with grey that were boldly assessing her in return.

His wide-legged no-nonsense stance set her heartbeat racing, and without thinking she snuck out her tongue to moisten lips that felt dryer than the paper she held between her fingers.

His eyes narrowed as they followed the movement, and Lily quickly cast her eyes downwards.

She pinched the bridge of her nose to ease the flash of pain that hammered behind her eyes, and blinked uncomprehendingly when a Mont Blanc pen was thrust in front of her face.

'Hurry up, Honey. I don't have all day.'

Lily wanted to remind him that she preferred Lily, but her throat was so tight she could barely swallow, let alone speak.

She grabbed the pen, flinching as her clumsy fingers collided with his, and scrawled her signature next to where he stabbed at the paper. Before she knew it the pages were whisked away, Tristan had grabbed her tote bag from Marine-man and he was ushering her out through the door with a firm guiding hand in the small of her back.

Lily stiffened away from the contact and rubbed her arms. He was well over six feet and seemed to dwarf her own five-foot-ten frame.

'If you're cold you should try wearing more clothing,' he snapped, hard eyes raking her body as if she were a foul piece of garbage.

Lily looked down at her white T-shirt, black leggings and black ballet flats.

'Ever heard of a bra, Honey?' His voice was silky, condescending, and Lily felt her breasts tighten as his gaze rested a little too long on her chest, her nipples firming against the fabric in a way she'd do anything to stop.

Lily was taken aback by his hostility, and it was all she could do not to cross her arms protectively over her body. She really wasn't up to dealing with any more animosity right now.

But she didn't say that. Instead she stared at the Windsor knot of his red tie and rubbed at the goosebumps that dotted her arms.

Tristan muttered something under his breath, shrugged out of his jacket, and draped it around her shoulders. She wanted to tell him she was fine, but before she could say anything he reached for her upper arm and propelled her down the long corridor, his clean, masculine scent blanketing her mind like a thick fog.

Tension bunched her stiff muscles, but she could hardly tell him to slow down when all she wanted to do was get as far away from the airport as possible. When he paused at the entrance to the duty-free hall Lily glanced up, feeling like an errant schoolgirl being dragged around by an enraged parent.

She tried to loosen his grip, put some distance between them, but he ignored her attempt, tightening his hold before marching her through the throng of passengers. It reminded her of a couple of occasions in the past when he'd stormed into nightclubs and goose-stepped herself and Jordana out. It had been mostly at her stepfather Frank Murphy's parties, and in hindsight Tristan had done the right thing making them leave at their age, but at the time Lily had been hopping mad.

She noticed the large steel doors leading to the arrivals hall and breathed a sigh of relief. Hopefully Jordana was waiting on the other side, and once through Lily could thank Tristan for his help and bid him farewell until the wedding.

Her nerves were shot, but the relief that washed through her at the thought of freedom was suddenly cut short as Tristan veered left and led her into one of the small, dimly lit bars that lined the cavernous concourse.

The bar was long and narrow, with booths lining one wall and a polished wooden bar with red padded bar stools along the other. Except for two business types, deep in conversation, and an elderly gent who looked as if he might tumble into his early-afternoon schooner, the place was empty.

Lily waited to find out what they were doing, and was surprised when Tristan ordered two whiskys, watching as he glared at the bartender, whose eyes had lingered a little too long in her direction.

As soon as he'd moved off to get their drinks Tristan turned to her, and Lily nearly recoiled at the feral anger icing his eyes.

'What the hell are you doing back in my sister's life?' he demanded, his voice harsh as he lowered it so only she could hear.

Lily did recoil then and stared at him mutely.

Six years just seemed to evaporate before her eyes,

and they might have been standing in his father's study again, where he'd accused her of something she hadn't done and called her a cheap slut.

Lily's eyes fell to his sensual mouth, now flattened into a thin line, and she quickly lowered them down the thick column of his tanned neck to rest once again on his silk tie. Looking at his mouth brought that devastating kiss to mind. She instantly reminded herself of his equally devastating rejection of her in an attempt to marshal her body's unexpected leap of excitement. How could she still feel so quivery over someone who had treated her so appallingly?

Tristan's tense silence seemed to envelop her, and she realised he was still waiting for her to respond to his rude question.

In all her mental imaginings of how this meeting between them would go this had not featured.

In one scenario she'd imagined they might be able to put the past behind them and become friends. Laugh over her silly teenage crush and his mistaken belief that she had set up the private party that had been splashed all over the internet. In that particular daydream she had raised her hand and said, *Please— don't give it another thought. It's over. It's in the past.*

But she didn't think that would play so well in this situation, and stupidly—so it now seemed—she had forgotten to prepare the whole busted-for-drugs-at-Heathrow scenario.

How remiss of her!

Now she had to ad lib, using a brain that wanted

to drool over him like a beginner art student viewing her first Rodin nude.

Only she was no longer an impressionable girl caught in the throes of her first crush, Lily reminded herself firmly. She was a mature woman in charge of her own life. And wasn't one of her goals on this trip to meet Tristan as an equal? To look at him, talk to him, and put the juvenile attraction that had plagued her so often in the company of other men to bed? Metaphorically speaking, of course.

'I was invited to the wedding,' she said as politely as possible, given that his harsh question had evoked exactly the opposite response.

'And what an error of judgement *that* was,' he sneered, 'I can't imagine what my sister was thinking.'

Lily frowned and glanced at the bartender, pouring whisky into two glasses, so that she wouldn't have to look at Tristan. Perhaps the best thing at this point would be to apologise for inconveniencing him and leave quick-smart.

She watched as Tristan picked up his glass and swallowed down the contents with a slight flick of his wrist; his brows drawing together when she made no attempt to do the same.

'Drink it. You look like you need it.'

'What I need is a soft bed,' she murmured, only realising how he'd taken her innocent comment when his eyebrows arched.

'If that's an invitation you can forget it,' he dismissed.

Invitation!

Lily expelled a rushed breath, and then inhaled just as hastily, wishing she hadn't as Tristan's virile and somehow familiar scent wound its way into her sinuses. She felt the shock of it curl through her body and suddenly felt too warm.

Her heart rate picked up, and before she could change the direction of her thoughts she was back at the kiss she had been trying so hard not to think about.

He'd been lean and muscle-packed where she'd pressed against him, impossibly hard, and hot colour stole into her face as she remembered her youthful eagerness in his embrace. Lord, perhaps she had even instigated it! How mortifying…Especially in light of the fact that she couldn't recall any other man's kisses quite so readily.

Calling herself every type of fool for indulging in such useless memories, she swiftly removed his jacket and handed it back to him.

Then she sat her tote bag on the stool behind her and pulled out her favourite oversized black knit cardigan. She put it on. Found her black-and-white Yankees baseball cap and pulled that on too. Turning back, she couldn't see much beyond Tristan's broad shoulders, but the last thing she wanted was to be stopped on the way out by fans or—heaven forbid—any lurking paparazzi.

She noticed his condescending glance and decided to ignore it.

She was getting more and more agitated by her own memories and his snippy attitude. Logically she knew he had every reason to be put out, but she hadn't done anything wrong. Would it really hurt him to be civil? After all, it wasn't as if *he* had just been interrogated for hours on end over something he hadn't done!

Lily tried to smile as she hoisted her bag onto her shoulder. 'So, anyway, thanks for helping today. I can see that you didn't really want to, but I appreciate it all the same.'

'I don't give a toss what you appreciate,' he grated. 'I can't believe you would have the gall to try something like this, given your history. What were you thinking? That you could go braless and swish that golden mane around and no one would care what you had in your bag?'

Lily's eyes flew to his. Did he seriously think she was guilty?

'Of course I wasn't thinking that!'

'Well, whatever you *were* thinking it didn't work.'

'How dare you?' Lily felt angry tears spring into her eyes at the injustice of his comment and blinked them back. 'I didn't know that stuff was in my bag, and I've already told you these are my travel clothes and I look perfectly respectable.'

His eyebrows arched. 'That's debatable. But I suppose I should be thankful you're not displaying as much skin as you usually do on your billboards.'

Lily didn't pretend to misunderstand him. Movie billboards were often more provocative than they needed to be, and most of her fellow actresses found it just as frustrating as she did.

Not that Tristan would believe that. It was clear he still thought the worst of her, just as he always had, and the sooner she was on her way the better.

She looked up to suggest exactly that, but was startled when he leaned in close, invading her space.

'Tell me, little Honey Blossom, have you ever been in a movie that required you to actually keep your clothes *on*?'

Lily bristled. She hadn't been called Honey Blossom since she was seven, and she'd been fully clothed in all but her first film. 'My name is Lily, as you well know, and your comments are not only insulting and incorrect, but completely outrageous.'

He cast her a bored smile and Lily's blood boiled. Of all the rude, insensitive—

'Just finish the damned drink, would you? I have work to do.'

Lily felt so tense her toes curled into her boots until they hurt. Enough was enough. Thankful or not, she didn't have to put up with his offensive remarks.

'I don't want your *damned* drink,' she returned icily, angling her chin and readjusting her cap. 'And I don't need your odious presence in my life for a second longer. Thank you for your assistance with my…unfortunate incident, but don't bother coming to say hello at the wedding. I assure you I won't be in the least offended.'

Lily gripped her bag tightly, and would have marched out with her head held high if Tristan hadn't made a slight move to block her.

She hesitated and looked at him uneasily.

'Pretty speech,' he drawled, 'but your *unfortunate incident* has landed you in my custody, and I give the orders now—not you.'

Lily's eyebrows shot up. 'Your *custody*?' She nearly laughed at the thought.

He evidently didn't like her response, because he leaned in even closer, his voice deadly soft. 'What? Did you think I would just ignore the conditions of your release and let you waltz out of here by yourself? You don't know me very well if you did.'

Lily edged back and felt the bar stool behind her thighs, a tremor of unease bumping down her spine. She hadn't read the release form at all, and had a feeling she was about to regret that.

'I didn't read it,' she admitted, sucking on the soft flesh of her upper lip—a nervous childhood gesture she'd never been able to master.

Tristan frowned down at her, and then must have realised she was serious because he had the gall to laugh. 'You're kidding.'

'I'm glad you find it funny,' she snapped, staring him down when his grim smile turned into a snarl.

'Now, *funny* is probably the last thing I think about

this situation—and here's why. You just signed documents that place you under my protective custody until you're either released—' his tone implied that was about as likely as buying property on another planet '—or charged with possession of narcotics.'

Lily felt dizzy and leaned heavily on the bar stool at her back. 'I don't understand…' She shook her head.

'What? You thought the evidence might up and magically disappear? I'm good, Honey, but I'm not that good.'

'No.' She waved her hand in front of her and briefly closed her eyes. 'The custody bit.'

'It's a form of house arrest.'

'I didn't know.'

'Now you do. And now I'm ready to leave.'

'No!' Her hand hovered between them and her voice quavered. 'Wait. Please. I… What does that mean, exactly?'

He looked at her as if she was a simpleton. 'It means that we're stuck with each other 24/7 for the foreseeable future, that's what it means.'

Lily blinked. 24/7 with this gorgeous, angry man…? No way. She pressed her fingertips to her aching forehead and ordered herself to think. Surely there was another solution.

'I can't stay with *you*!' She blurted out before her thoughts were properly in order.

His eyes sparkled into hers, as hard as polished

gemstones. 'Believe me, the thought couldn't be more abhorrent to you than it is to me.'

'But you should have told me!'

'You should have read the paperwork,' he dismissed.

He was right, and she hated that. Only it was because of him that she hadn't read it in the first place.

'You crowded me and told me to hurry.'

'So now it's my fault?' he snapped.

'I wasn't blaming you.' She swiped a hand across her brow. This was terrible. 'But if you had warned me about what I was signing I wouldn't have done so!'

He went still, his over-long tawny mane and square jaw giving the impression of a fully grown male lion that had just scented danger.

'Warned you?'

Too late Lily realised he'd taken her comment as an insult.

'And what exactly would you have done, hmm? Do tell.'

Lily pressed her lips together at his snide tone and tried not to notice how imposing he was, with his hands on his hips drawing his shoulders even wider. If she'd thought he hated her six years ago it was nothing compared to the contempt he clearly felt for her now.

And she wasn't so much looking to put the past behind her any more as she was in burying it in a six-foot-deep hole! 'I—I would have looked for an alternative,' she stuttered. 'Brainstormed other options.'

'Brainstormed other options?' He snorted and shook his head, as if the very notion was ludicrous. 'We're not in a movie rehearsal now, Honey!'

Lily's heart thudded heavily in her chest. If he called her Honey one more time she might actually hit him. She took a deep, steadying breath and tried to remember that he felt he had a right to be angry, and that maybe, if their situations were reversed, she would feel the same way.

No, she wouldn't. She'd be too worried for the other person to treat them so—so…indignantly.

'Listen—' she began, only to have her words cut off when he pushed off his bar stool and crowded her back against her own.

'No. *You* listen,' he bit out softly. 'You don't have a choice here. You're no longer in charge. I am. And if you don't like it I'll give you another option. It's called a prison cell. You want it—it's back that way.' He jerked his chin towards the entrance of the bar, his eyes never leaving hers.

Lily blanched. Lord, he was arrogant.

'I didn't do it,' she enunciated, trying to keep her voice low.

'Tell it to the judge, sweetheart, because I'm not interested in hearing your protestations of innocence.'

'Don't patronise me, Tristan. I'm not a child.'

'Then stop acting like one.'

'Damn you, I have rights.'

'No, you *had* rights.' His tone was soft, but merciless. 'You gave up those rights the minute you waltzed through Heathrow carrying a bag full of narcotics. Your rights belong to me now, and when I say jump I expect you to ask how high.'

Lily froze. He had some nerve. 'In your dreams,' she scoffed, now just as angry as he was.

CHAPTER THREE

No, TRISTAN thought disgustedly, when he dreamt of her she was not jumping up and down; she was usually naked, her lithe body spread out over his bed, and her soft mouth was begging him to take her. But this was no dream, and right now making love to her couldn't be further from his mind.

Kissing that insolent curl from her luscious mouth—now, *that* was closer. But completely giving in to the insane desire that still uncomfortably rode his back—no. Not in this lifetime.

Not that he was at all surprised to find himself still attracted to her. Hell, she looked even better now than she had six years ago—if that was actually possible.

Even the bartender was having trouble keeping his distance—and not just because he'd probably recognised her face. Tristan doubted he'd be ogling any other actress with his tongue hanging out of his mouth, and there were many far more worthy of a second glance than this sexy little troublemaker.

No, the bartender was staring because Lily Wild looked like every man's secret fantasy come to life—

even with those dark smudges beneath those wide purple eyes. But she damned well wasn't his. Not this time.

He should have just said no to Jordana, he realised distractedly. Should have made up a story about how it couldn't be done.

But he had too much integrity to lie, and in the end a close friend who specialised in criminal law had pulled a rabbit from a hat and here they were. But only by the grace of some clapped-out piece of nineteenth-century legislation that he would recommend be amended at the next parliamentary sitting.

'Did you hear me, Tristan?' she prompted, her glorious eyes flashing with unconcealed irritation. 'I won't let you bully me like you did once before.'

Tristan cast her the withering glance that he usually reserved for the seediest of his courtroom opponents.

Oh, he'd heard her all right, but she had no choice in the matter, and the sooner she got that through her thick, beautiful skull the better.

'Don't push me, Lily,' he grated warningly, and saw her teeth clench.

Her hands were fisted by her sides and he knew she probably wanted to thump him. Despite himself he admired her temerity. Most women in her position—hell, most *men*—would be grovelling or backing away, or both. Instead this little spitfire was arguing the toss, as if she might actually choose jail over him.

'Then don't push *me*!' she returned hotly.

He looked at her and tried to remind himself that he was a first-rate lawyer who never let emotion govern his actions. 'You signed the contract. Deal with it,' he said curtly.

She slapped her hands on her hips, the movement dragging her oversized cardigan open and bringing his attention back to her full, unbound breasts. 'I told you—I didn't know what I was signing,' she declared, as if that might actually make a difference.

Yeah, yeah—just as she didn't know how the drugs ended up in her bag. He had yet to come across a criminal who actually admitted any form of guilt, and her vehement denial was boringly predictable.

He noticed that the two businessmen who earlier had been deep in conversation were now stealing surreptitious glances at her. Not that he couldn't appreciate what they were looking at: tousled pearl-blond hair, soft, kissable lips, a mouthwatering silhouette, and legs that went all the way into next week.

They'd looked even longer coming down his parents' staircase at Jo's eighteenth party, in a tiny dress and designer heels. And just like that he was back at Hillesden Abbey, the family estate, at the precise moment she had approached him.

'Hey, wanna dance?' she'd invited, standing before him in a silver mini-dress that clung in all the right places, hip cocked, bee-stung pout covered in war paint.

He'd declined, of course. Just looking at her had

stirred up a dark lust inside him that, at seventeen, she had been way too young to handle.

'But you danced with Jordana,' she'd complained, fluttering ridiculously long eyelashes like a woman on the make. 'And the girl with the blue dress.'

'That's right.' His friend Gabriel had elbowed him. 'You did.'

'So? What about it?' Lily had shifted her weight to her other hip, her dress riding up just that tiny bit more, head tilted in artful provocation.

He'd been about to refuse again, but Gabriel had interrupted and said *he'd* dance with her if Tristan wouldn't, and for some reason that had got his back up.

He'd thrown his friend a baleful glare before focusing on Lily. 'Let's go.'

She'd smiled her now famous million dollar smile at Gabriel and Tristan had gritted his teeth and followed her onto the dance floor.

As if on cue the music had turned dreamy and he'd almost changed his mind. Then she'd turned that million dollar number his way, stepped into his arms, and he'd no longer had a mind to change.

'It's a great party, isn't it?' she'd murmured.

'Yes,' he'd agreed.

'This is nice,' she'd prompted.

'Yes,' he'd agreed.

'Are you having a good time?'

Not any more; not with his self-control unravelling with each breathy little question.

He remembered he'd been so focused on not pulling her in close that he failed to notice when *she* had moved in on *him*. Then he'd felt the slide of her bare thigh between his jean-clad legs and the thrust of her pert breasts against the wall of his chest and self-control had become a foreign concept.

His hand had tightened on her hip to push her back, but she'd gripped his shoulder and looked at him with such unguarded innocence his heart had skipped a beat, and almost of its own accord his hand had slid around to the sweet indentation at the small of her back.

Her breath had hitched and when she'd stumbled he'd caught her against him. Her body had instantly moulded to his as if she was unable to hold herself upright. And he'd been unable to hide his physical reaction from her. His body had been gripped in a fever of desire: heart pounding, body aching and warning bells clanging so loudly in his head it was a wonder he'd been able to think at all.

He'd stupidly danced her into a secluded corner, with every intention of reprimanding her and telling her he didn't *do* girls barely out of nappies, but she'd quivered in the circle of his arms, lips delicately parted, and he'd fused his mouth with hers before he'd even known what he was about.

The bolt of pure heat that had hit his groin at the contact had almost unmanned him.

Before he'd known it he'd had one hand tangled in her golden mane, the other curved over her bottom and his tongue deep in her mouth, his lips demanding a response she had been more than happy to give.

He'd completely lost all sense of where he was, and hours could have flown by before a hand had circumspectly tapped him on the shoulder.

Thomas, the family butler, had stood behind him, seemingly mesmerised by the imported mirror balls suspended above the dance floor.

Apparently his father required his presence most urgently.

For a second Lily's dazed disappointment had only been outweighed by his own. Then he'd realised what he'd nearly done and been appalled at himself. She was his little sister's friend, and the erotic images playing through his mind were highly inappropriate.

He remembered he'd abruptly released her and curtly told her not to bother him again, that he wasn't interested in babies. And then she'd punished him by attaching herself to some Armani suit for the rest of the night like ivy on a brick wall.

One of the businessmen hooted a laugh, and the sound broke Tristan's unwanted reverie.

He closed his eyes briefly to recompose himself, and then made the mistake of glancing into the mirror behind the bar—where his gaze collided with Lily's.

For a split second something hot and primal arced between them, and then the pink tip of her tongue snuck out to douse her full lower lip and just like that he was hard again.

Damn. Had she done that on purpose? Had she known what he'd been thinking about?

He blinked slowly and turned his gaze as hard as his groin. He wasn't an idiot, and he wasn't going to let her use that come-hither look she'd probably learned in the cradle to manipulate him. The sooner she figured that out, the better for the both of them.

'I don't care what you did or didn't know. You signed the forms and now we're leaving.'

'Wait.' She put her hand out to touch him and then snatched it back just as quickly.

His jaw clenched. 'What now?'

'We need to sort this out.'

He picked his jacket up off the stool and shrugged into it. 'It's sorted. I'm in charge. You're not. So let's go.'

'Look, I know you're angry—'

'Is that what I am?' he mocked.

'But,' she continued determinedly, 'I didn't know I had that…stuff in my bag.' Her voice was barely above a whisper. 'And I'm not going with you until I know what happens next.'

Tristan glanced at the ceiling, hoping some divine force would penetrate it and put him out of his misery. He knew she had a headache. He'd known the minute he'd seen her. And now she was giving him one.

'You've got to be kidding me,' he groaned.

'No, I'm not. I mean it, Tristan; I won't let you push me around like you did six years ago. Back then—'

'Oh, cut the theatrics, Honey. There's no camera to turn it on for here.'

'Lily.'

He stared at her for a beat.

'And I'm not—'

Tristan glared at her and cut her off. 'You think I like this any more than you do? You think I didn't rack my brain to come up with an alternative? I have just involved a good friend of mine to get you out of this mess and all you can do is act the injured innocent. *You* broke the law, not me, so stop behaving like I'm the bad guy here.'

Lily seemed to lose a little steam over that. 'A friend?' she whispered.

'What? You thought I could just stroll up here myself and demand your release? I'm flattered you think I have that much power.'

Tristan glanced around the bar and saw that more passengers had entered. They were getting far more attention than he was comfortable with.

'He won't go to the press, will he?' she asked.

Tristan shook his head. 'So typical of you to be worried about yourself.'

'I wasn't worrying about myself,' she snapped. 'I was thinking about how this might impact Jordana's wedding if it gets out.'

'A bit late to think about that now. But, no, he won't say anything. He has discretion and integrity—words you'd need to look up in a dictionary to learn the meaning of.' He shook his head at the improbability of the whole situation. 'For God's sake, it's not as if you couldn't get a fix here if you were so desperate.'

She looked at him from under her cap. 'Whatever happened to being innocent in this country until proven guilty?'

'Being caught with drugs in your bag sort of makes that a moot point,' he scoffed.

Lily's chin jutted forward. 'Aren't lawyers supposed to be a little more objective with their clients?'

'I'm not your lawyer.'

'What are you, then? My white knight?'

A muscle ticked in his jaw. 'I'm doing Jordana a favour.'

'Ah, yes. The big brother routine,' she mocked. 'I seem to recall you really enjoy that. It must have made you feel valued—rescuing Jordana from my disreputable company all those years ago.'

She wrapped her arms around her torso in a defensive gesture that pinched something inside him, but he refused to soften towards her. He had no respect for people who created a demand for drugs and hurt those around them by using, and all today had done was confirm his father's view that Lily Wild was bad news just waiting to happen.

'It's just a pity I didn't nip your friendship in the bud sooner. I could have saved my family a lot of embarrassment.'

That seemed to take the wind out of her sails and he almost felt bad when her shoulders slumped.

'So what happens now? Where will I be staying?' she asked.

Tristan pulled a wad of notes from his pocket and threw some on the bar. 'We'll discuss the ground rules later.'

'I'd like to talk about them now.'

He turned to her, what little patience he'd started with completely gone. 'If I have to pick you up and cart you out of here I will,' he warned softly.

Her eyes widened. 'You wouldn't dare.'

Tristan crowded her back against the bar stool again. 'Try me.'

She inhaled a shaky breath and put her hand up between them. 'Don't touch me.'

Touch her? He hadn't really intended to, but now, as his gaze swept down her curvy body, he realised that he wanted to. Badly. He wanted to push aside that cardigan, slide his hand around her waist and pull her up against him until there was no sign of daylight between them. Until she melted into him as she had done six years ago.

'Then co-operate,' he snarled, crowding even closer and perversely enjoying her agitated backwards movement. It wouldn't hurt her to be a little afraid of him. Might make sure she kept her distance this time.

'I'm trying to.'

Her eyes flashed, and the leather creaked as she

shifted as far back on the stool as she could, her monstrosity of a bag perched on her lap between them.

Tristan leaned forward and hooked his foot on her bar stool, jerking it forward so she was forced back into his space. He caught her off guard, and his bicep flexed as she threw her hand out to balance herself. Her breath caught and her eyes flew to his.

'No, you're not. You're trying to bug me.' He watched as colour winged into her face, his eyes narrowing as she snatched her hand back from his arm. 'And it's working.'

She raised her chin. 'I don't like your controlling attitude.'

He stilled, and their eyes locked in a battle of wills: hers bright and belligerent, his surprised but determined. His nostrils flared as he breathed her in deep. She smelled of roses and springtime and he had to fight the instinct to keep inhaling her.

They were so close he could see the flawless, luminescent quality of her skin—a gift from her Nordic heritage—and her thick, sooty lashes, as long as a spider's legs, nearly touching her arched brow. His eyes turned hot before he was able to blank them out, and her breath stalled as she caught the heat.

He stopped breathing himself and felt the blood throb powerfully through his body. For a split second he forgot what they were doing here. Time stood still. But before he could wrap his hand around her slender neck and bring her mouth to his she blinked and lowered her eyes.

Tristan exhaled, his anger all the stronger because of the unwanted sexual tension that lay between them like a living thing.

'Do you really think I care?' he snapped. 'When I first heard you were coming to Jo's wedding I didn't even intend to say hello. Now I find that hello is the least of my problems, and I can assure you I will *not* spend the next eight days arguing every single point with you. So if—'

'Fine.' She cupped her hand over her forehead and winced.

He knew what she meant, but he was insulted by her attitude and wanted to hear her say it.

'Fine what? Fine, you want to come with me? Or fine, you want me to take you back to Customs?'

She raised her head and he waited. The smudges under her eyes looked darker, and her skin had lost even more colour.

'Oh, to hell with it.' He straightened and held his hand out to her. She took it, without argument, and he realised that the shock of the morning was finally starting to set in—or maybe she'd been in shock the whole time.

Her fingers were icy in his, and he shrugged out of his jacket once again and pulled it around her. She squirmed as if to push it off, and her eyes jerked to his when he grabbed her upper arms and dragged her close.

'Co-operate,' he growled, pleased when she stilled.

'You never say please.' She sniffed.

Hell, she was still trying to call the shots. He kept his eyes locked on hers, because if they dropped to her mouth he knew he'd taste her. He was hard and he was angry, and the adrenaline pumping through his veins was pushing his self-control to its outer limits.

'Please,' he grated after a long, tense pause. 'Now, can you walk?'

'Of course.' She gripped her bag and swayed when he released his hold on her.

He knew it would be a mistake on so many levels, but before he could think twice he scooped her into his arms and strode out of the bar.

She started against him, but he'd had enough. 'Don't say a goddamned word and don't look around. The last thing I need is for someone else to recognise you.'

And just like that she relaxed and turned her head into his shoulder, her sweet scent filling his every breath.

The cool breeze was a welcome relief as he exited the terminal and headed down the rank of dark cars until he found Bert.

His chauffer nodded and held the rear door open, but just as Tristan was about to toss Lily inside she laid the flat of her hand against his chest and looked up through sleepy eyes.

'My luggage...' she murmured.

Tristan's chest contracted against the hot brand of her touch.

'Taken care of,' he growled, wishing the unbearable physical attraction he still felt for this woman could be just as easily dealt with.

CHAPTER FOUR

LILY collapsed back against the luxuriant leather car seat and closed her eyes, trying to equalise her pounding heart rate. Her head hurt and she felt shivery all over. She didn't know if it was remembering her previous attraction to Tristan that had brought it screaming to the fore, or the man himself, but she was unable to deny the sweet feeling of desire that had pooled low in her pelvis when he'd held her in his arms and looked at her as if he wanted to kiss her.

Kiss her? *Ha!* Shake her, more like it. Especially given how much he still disliked her.

As she did him.

Actually, now that she thought about it, her physical response was probably due to emotional tiredness and stress making her super-sensitive to her surroundings and nothing to do with Tristan at all. How could it be when he immediately assumed that she was guilty? When he clearly thought she was lower than dirt?

His cold arrogance fired her blood and made her want to fall back on all her juvenile responses to criticism. Responses that had seen her play up to the negative attention her celebrity lineage provoked by flipping the press the bird, wearing either provocative or grungy clothing, depending on her mood, and pretending she was drunk when she wasn't.

Nowadays she preferred to ignore any bad press or unfair comparisons with her parents' hedonistic lifestyles, and just live her life according to her own expectations rather than other people's. It worked better, to a certain extent, although she knew she'd never truly be able to outrun the shadow of who her parents had been.

Hanny Forsberg, her mother, had arrived in England poor and beautiful and on Page Three before she had found a place to live, and Johnny Wild, her father, had been a rough Norfolk lad with a raw musical talent and a hunger for success and women in equal measure.

Both had thrived on their fame and the attention it engendered, and after Lily was born they had just added her to their lifestyle—palming her off on whichever one wasn't working and treating her like a fashion accessory long before it had become hip to do so.

The camera flashes and constant attention had scared her as a child, and even now Lily hated that she always felt as if she was living under the sullied banner of her parents' combined notoriety. But none of that had been enough to put her off when her own creativity and natural talent had led her down the acting career path. Lily just tried as best she could to take roles that didn't immediately provoke comparisons between herself and her parents—though as to that she could play a cross-dressing homosexual male and probably still be compared to her mother!

Sighing heavily, and wishing that one of her directors was going to call 'cut' on a day from hell, Lily turned to stare out at the passing landscape she hadn't seen for so long.

Unfortunately the rows of shop fronts and Victorian terraces soon made her head throb, and she was forced to close her eyes and listen to the sound of Tristan texting on his smartphone instead. A thousand questions were winging through her mind—none of which, she knew, Tristan would feel inclined to answer.

For a moment she contemplated pulling the script she had promised to read from her bag, but that would no doubt make the headache worse so she left it there.

No great hardship, since she didn't want to read it anyway. She had no interest in starring in a theatrical production about her parents, no matter how talented the writer-director was.

She'd nearly scoffed out loud at the notion.

As if she'd feed the gossipmongers and provoke more annoying comparisons to her mother by actually *playing* her in a drama. Lord, she'd never hear the end of it. The only reason she was pretending to consider the idea was a favour to a friend.

Her mouth twisted as she imagined the look on

Tristan's face if he knew about the role. No doubt he'd think her perfect to play a lost, drug-addled model craving love and attention from a man who had probably put the word *playboy* in the dictionary.

In fact it was ironic, really, that the only man Lily had ever thought herself to be in love with was almost as big a playboy as her father! Not that she'd fully comprehended Tristan's reputation as a seventeen-year-old. Back then she'd known only that women fell for him like pebbles tossed into a pond, but she hadn't given it much thought.

Now she was almost glad that he'd rejected her gauche overtures, because if he hadn't she'd surely have become just another notch on his bedpost. And if she *was* anything like her mother that would have meant she'd have fallen for him all the harder.

Lily removed her cap and rubbed her forehead, glancing briefly at Tristan, slashing his red pen through a document he was reading. If she tried to interrupt him now to discuss her house arrest he'd no doubt bite her head off. Still...

'I take it you won't be put out if I don't feel up to making conversation right now?' she queried innocuously, smiling brightly when he looked at her as if she had two heads. 'Thought not,' she mumbled.

Suddenly she was feeling drained, and not up to fighting with him anyway, so it was a good thing he'd ignored her taunt. A taunt she shouldn't have made in the first place. Never prod a sleeping tiger...wasn't that the adage? Especially when you were in the same cage as him!

Lily leaned back against the plush leather headrest and closed her eyes. The manly scent from Tristan's jacket imbued her with a delicious and oddly peaceful lassitude, and she tried to pretend none of this was happening.

Cheeky minx! She knew he didn't want to talk. He couldn't have made it any plainer. He slashed another line through the report he was reading and realised he'd marked up the wrong section. Damn her.

She sighed, and he wondered if she knew the effect she was having on his concentration, but when he glanced up it was to find she'd fallen asleep.

She looked so fragile, swamped in his jacket, her blonde hair spilling over the dark fabric like a silvery web.

He knew when he got it back it would smell like something from his late mother's garden, and made a mental note to have his housekeeper immediately launder it. Then he realised the direction of his thoughts and frowned.

He was supposed to be focused on work. Not contemplating Lily and her hurt expression when he'd cut off her attempts to explain her situation earlier.

He didn't want to get caught up in her lies, and he had taken the view that the less she said the better for both of them. She had a way of getting under his skin, and for an insanely brief moment back in the bar, when her eyes had teared up, he'd wanted to reach out and tell her that everything would be all right. Which was ridiculous.

It wasn't his job to fix her situation. His job—if you could call it that—was to keep her out of trouble until Jordana's wedding and find out any relevant information that might lead to her—or someone else's—arrest.

It was not to make friends with her, or to make empty promises. And it certainly wasn't to kiss her as he had wanted to do. He shook his head. Maybe he really had taken leave of his senses getting involved with this. Stuart, the friend and colleague who had helped him find the loophole in the law that had placed her into his custody, had seemed to think so.

'Are you sure you know what you're doing, Chief?' he'd asked, after the deal had been sealed.

'When have you ever needed to ask me that?'

His friend had raised an eyebrow at his surly tone and Tristan had known what was coming.

'Never. But if she's guilty and people question your involvement it could ruin your legal career. Not to mention drag your family name through the mud again.'

'I know what I'm doing,' he'd said. But he didn't. Not really.

What he *did* know was that he was still as strongly attracted to her as he had been six years ago. Not that he was going to do anything about it. He would never get involved with a drug-user.

His mother had been one—although not a recreational user, like Lily and her ilk. His mother had taken a plethora of prescription meds for everything from dieting to depression, but the effect was the same: personality changes, mood swings, and eventually death when she had driven her car into a tree.

She had never been an easy woman to love. A shop girl with her eye on the big prize, she had married his father for his title and, from what Tristan could tell, had spent most of their life together complaining on the one hand that he worked too hard and on the other that the Abbey was too old for her tastes. His father had done his best, but in the end it hadn't been enough, and she'd left after a blazing row Tristan still wished he hadn't overheard. His father had been gutted, and for a while lost to his children, and Tristan had vowed then that he would never fall that deeply under a woman's spell.

He expelled a harsh breath. He was thirty-two years old and in the prime of his life. He had an international law firm and a property portfolio that spanned four continents, good friends and enough money to last several lifetimes—even with the amount he gave away to charity. His personal life had become a little mundane lately, it was true, but he didn't really know what to do about that.

Jordana thought it was because he chose unsuitable women most of the time, and if he did date someone 'worthy' he ended the relationship before it began. Which was true enough. Experience had taught him that after a certain time a woman started expecting more from a man. Started wanting to talk about love and commitment. And after one particularly virulent model had sold her story to the tabloids he had made sure his affairs remained short and sweet. Very sweet and very short.

He knew he'd probably marry one day, because it was expected, but love wouldn't play a part in his choice of a wife. When he was ready—if he ever was—he'd choose someone from his world, who understood the demands of his lifestyle. Someone logical and pragmatic like he was.

Lily made a noise in her sleep and Tristan flicked a glance at her, wincing as her head dropped sideways and butted up against the glass window. Someone the opposite of this woman.

She whimpered and jerked upright in her sleep, but didn't waken, and Tristan watched the cycle start to repeat itself. That couldn't be good for her headache.

Not that he cared. He didn't. She was the reason memories from the past were crowding in and clouding his normally clear thinking, and he resented the hell out of her for it.

But just as her head was about to bump the window again he cursed and moved to her side, to move her along the seat. She flopped against his shoulder and snuggled into his arm, her silky hair brushing against his cheek, giving him pause. He felt the warmth of her breath through his shirt and went still when she made a soft, almost purring sound in the back of her throat; his traitorous body responded predictably.

If he were to move back to his side now she might wake up and, frankly, he could do without her peppering him with the questions he'd seen hovering on her lips while he'd been trying to work.

She made another pained whimper and he looked down to see a frown marring her pale forehead.

Oh, for the love of God.

He blew out a breath and lifted his free hand to her hairline, stroked her brow. The frown eased instantly from her forehead and transferred to his own. If he wasn't careful this whole situation could get seriously out of hand. He could just feel it.

Five minutes. He'd give her five minutes and then he'd move. Get back to the waiting e-mails on his smartphone.

Twenty minutes later, just as he was about to ease his fingers from her tangled tresses, his chauffeur announced that the car had stopped. Well, of course he'd noticed.

'Drive us to the rear entrance, Bert,' he said, trying to rouse Lily. She rubbed her soft cheek against his palm in such a trusting gesture his chest tightened.

God, she really was a stunning woman.

How could someone born looking like she did throw it all away on drugs? He knew she must have struggled, losing both her parents at a young age, but still—they all had their crosses to bear. What made some people rise above the cards life dealt them while others sank into the mire?

According to Jordana, Lily was sensible, reserved and down to earth. Yeah, and he was the Wizard of Oz.

'You okay, Boss?' Bert asked, concern shadowing his voice.

Great. He hadn't noticed the car had pulled up again. He had to stop thinking of Lily as a desirable woman before it was no longer important that he neither liked nor respected her.

'Never better.' He exhaled, manoeuvring himself out of the car and effortlessly lifting the comatose woman into his arms. She stirred, but instantly re-settled against him. No doubt a combination of shock and jet lag was laying her out cold.

A security guard opened the glass-plated door to his building, looking for all the world as if there was nothing out of place in his boss carrying an uncon-scious woman towards the service lift.

'Nice afternoon, sir.'

Tristan grunted in return, flexing his arms under Lily's dead weight.

He exited the lift and strode towards his office throwing a 'don't ask' look at his ever-efficient sec-retary as she hurried around her desk to push his door open for him.

'Hold all my calls,' he instructed Kate, before kick-ing the door closed with his heel.

He tumbled Lily gently down onto the white leather

sofa in his office and she immediately curled into a fetal position, pulling his jacket more tightly around her body while she slept.

Scratch laundering it, he thought. He'd just throw the bloody thing away.

CHAPTER FIVE

LILY was hot. Too hot. And something was tugging on her. Pulling her down. Jonah?

She blinked and tried to focus, and found herself lying in an unfamiliar room.

'Missing your boyfriend already, Honey?' An aggravated male voice she instantly recognised drawled from far away.

Lily tentatively raised herself up on her elbow to find Tristan seated behind a large desk strewn with leatherbound books and reams of paper.

For a moment she just stared at him in a daze, unconsciously registering his dark frown. Then the events of the morning started replaying through her mind like a silent movie on fast forward.

The flight, the drugs, the interrogation, Tristan—

'You called his name,' he prompted. 'A number of times.'

Whose name?

Lily didn't know what he was talking about. She didn't have a lover and never had. She smoothed her fingers over her flushed face and wiped the edges of her mouth. It felt suspiciously as if she had drooled. *Urgh!* She was grimy and sweaty, as if she'd been asleep for days. Of course she hadn't been—had she?

Lily peered at Tristan more closely and noticed the same white shirt he'd worn earlier, the sleeves now rolled to reveal muscular bronzed forearms. The same red tie hanging loosely around his neck and the top button of his shirt was undone. Okay, still Friday. Thank heavens. She glanced around his impressively large and impressively messy office.

For some reason she had expected someone so controlling to be a neat freak, but his desk was barely visible behind small towers of black, green and red legal tomes and spiral-bound notebooks. A set of inlaid bookcases lined half of one wall, with books stacked vertically and horizontally in a slapdash manner, and what looked like an original Klimt dominated another.

And that surprised her as well. Klimt had a soft, almost magical quality to his work, and that didn't fit her image of Tristan at all.

'It's an investment,' he said, as if he could read her mind. 'So who is he to you?' Tristan repeated, pulling her eyes back to his.

'Gustav Klimt?'

Tristan made an impatient sound. 'The loser whose name you were chanting in your sleep.'

Lily shook her head, realising one of the reasons she felt so hot was because she still wore Tristan's jacket. Removing it quickly, she placed it on the seat beside her and met his scornful gaze. 'I don't know who you're— Oh, Jonah!'

'He'd no doubt be upset to find himself so easily dismissed from your memory. But then with so many lovers on the go how can a modern girl be expected to keep up?'

Lily's brow pleated as she gazed at him. No improvement in his mood, then. Wonderful.

And as for his disparaging comments about her so-called lovers—the press reported she was in a relationship every time she so much as shared a taxi with a member of the opposite sex, so really he could be talking about any number of men.

She was just about to tell him she didn't appreciate his sarcasm when he held up a manila folder, a look of contempt crossing his face.

'I've had a report done on you.'

Of course he had.

'Ever considered going directly to the source?' she suggested sweetly. 'Probably save you a lot in investigators' fees.'

Tristan tapped his pen against his desk. 'I find investigators far more enlightening than "the source".'

'How nice for you.'

'For example, you're currently living with Cliff Harris...'

A dear friend who had moved into her spare room due to financial problems.

'A lovely man.' She smiled thinly.

'...while you've been photographed cosying up to that effeminate sculptor Piers Bond.'

Lily had been to a few gallery openings with Piers, and Tristan was right—he was effeminate.

'A very talented artist,' she commented.

'And presumably sleeping with that dolly boy in Thailand behind both their backs?'

Lily suppressed her usually slow to rise temper and threw him her best Mona Lisa smile. A smile she had perfected long ago that said everything and nothing all at the same time.

'Grip,' she corrected with forced pleasantness. 'He's called a dolly grip.'

'He's also called a junkie.'

'Jonah *once* had a drug problem; he doesn't any more.'

'Well, you should know. You've been photographed going in and out of that New York rehab clinic with him enough times.'

Also true. She volunteered there when she could, which was how she'd met Jonah. She just hoped Tristan didn't know about the director's marriage she was supposed to have broken up while working on a film the year before. But since it had been all through the papers...

'And Guy Jeffrey's marriage? Or is that so far back you can't remember your part in that particular melo-drama?'

Great. He probably knew her shoe size as well.

'My, your man *is* thorough,' she complimented

dryly. 'But do you think I might visit the bathroom before you remind me about the rest of my debauched lifestyle? I don't think I can hang on till tomorrow.'

Tristan scowled at her from beneath straight brows, and if the situation hadn't been so awful she might have laughed. Might have.

She picked up her tote bag from the floor and grimaced as she realised she felt as if she was requesting a permission slip from the school principal when she had to ask for directions to the bathroom.

Tristan nodded towards a door at the rear of his office. 'Leave the bag,' he ordered, returning his focus to his computer screen.

'Why?'

'Because I said so.'

Rude, horrible, insufferable... He raised his eyes and locked them with hers. His gave nothing away about how he was feeling while she knew hers were shooting daggers.

She suspected she knew why he wanted her to leave it. She suspected he was trying to show her who was boss. Either that or he thought she'd been able to magic some more drugs into her bag after it had been searched by Customs. But, whatever his reasoning, he'd now succeeded in making her angry again.

She planted her hands on her hips, prepared to stare him down. 'There's nothing in it.'

He leaned back in his chair and regarded her as a

predator might regard lunch, and goosebumps rose up along her arms. 'Then you won't mind leaving it.'

Lily felt her mouth tighten. No, but she wouldn't mind braining him with it either—and damn him if he didn't know it.

She stalked towards him, her narrowed eyes holding his, and before she could think better of it up-ended the entire contents of her tote onto his desk. He couldn't hide his start of surprise, and Lily felt inordinately pleased at having knocked him off his arrogant perch.

'Careful.' She cast him her best Hollywood smile before swinging round towards the bathroom. 'I left a King Cobra in there somewhere, and it's trained to attack obnoxious lawyers.'

As parting shots went she thought it was rather good, but his unexpected chuckle set her teeth on edge. And if she was honest she was a bit worried she'd never find her favourite lipstick again in amongst all the rubble on his desk.

His bathroom was state-of-the-art, with slate-grey tiles and an enormous plate-glass shower stall. Lily would almost kill for a shower, but the thought of putting on her smelly travel clothes afterwards was not appealing. Plus Tristan was in the other room, and she didn't want to risk that he might walk in on her. She didn't think she could cope.

A sudden image of him naked and soapy, with water streaming off the lean angles and hard planes of his body, crowding her back against the slippery tiles pervaded her senses and made her feel light-headed. She wondered if he had an all-over tan, and then pulled a face at the image of male perfection that bombarded her. He probably had a very small penis, she thought, grinning at her wan complexion. It would only be fair.

But then she recalled the feel of his hard body pressed into hers in the secluded corner of that long-ago dance floor and knew he wasn't small. Far from it.

She wouldn't ruin her mood by thinking about that. Somehow tipping her bag upside down on Tristan's desk had alleviated her anger and lifted her spirits considerably.

She splashed cold water on her cheeks and poked at the dark circles under her eyes. She looked a mess. And her hair was unusually knotty around her temples. A vague memory of soothing fingers stroking her scalp came to mind and she realised at the same time that her headache was gone. Had he stroked her? Soothed her?

The comforting gesture didn't fit his harsh attitude, but she was secretly thrilled that he might have done it.

Thrilled? No. She shook her head at her reflection. Thoughts like that led to nothing but trouble, and hadn't he already made it completely clear that he detested every minute he had to spend with her? And didn't she feel exactly the same way? The man was rude, arrogant and obnoxious, to say the least.

She blew out a noisy breath and pulled her hair into a rough ponytail, securing it with the band she kept around her wrist for just such purposes—a habit that made Jordana shudder. But Lily had never been one for fashion and clothing, like Jordana. Which was probably why Jordana was a buyer for women's wear at a leading department store and Lily wore just about anything she recommended.

Lily turned towards the door and paused with her hand on the brass knob. She was almost afraid to return to the lion's den.

Then she chastised herself for her feebleness.

No doubt Tristan was just planning to lay down the law. Tell her he wanted absolute silence and co-operation again. And if he did she wouldn't argue. The less they had to do with each other the better.

Sure, she had questions, but perhaps it was better to try and stifle them. She'd soon find out what was going to happen, and as much as the thought of being at his mercy made her skin crawl what choice did she really have right now?

Yes, that would be the approach to take. Polite, but aloof. Mind her own business and hope he minded his as well.

Tristan regarded Lily coolly as she walked back into his office. She'd put her hair up, which made her look more unkempt than when she'd first woken up—and incredibly cute. A fact he found hard to believe when he usually preferred women well-mannered, well-bred and well-groomed.

He was still smarting from having lowered himself to question her about her lovers before, like some jealous boyfriend, and wouldn't have minded if she'd spent the rest of the afternoon in the bathroom. All the better for him to get some actual work done.

But she hadn't, and now her eyes alighted on the refreshments his secretary had just placed on his desk. He knew she must be hungry, because he doubted the customs officers had made it a priority to feed her earlier today.

He suppressed a grin when he saw her glance surreptitiously around for her bag. Much as he hated to admit it, he admired her spunk.

'No, I didn't bin it,' he said conversationally. 'Although there wasn't much in there worth keeping apart from a miniature pair of black panties.'

Her eyes flew to his and he had to wonder why he'd said that. It had gone totally against his intention to direct her to the sofa and tell her to keep quiet.

Her mouth gaped with embarrassment and he almost felt sorry for her. She'd obviously forgotten they were in there.

Then she recovered and sauntered across the room. 'I'm not sure they're your size, but you're welcome to keep them.'

'I generally like to take them off women, not put them on,' he purred, enjoying the way her eyes widened before lancing him with a knowing look.

'So I've heard,' she rejoined. 'But I was referring to your personal use, not…' Her pouty lips tightened and she looked flustered, dropping her gaze to the assortment of cups in front of her. 'Never mind. I take it one of these is mine?'

'Yes. Take your pick. I didn't know if you preferred coffee or tea so I ordered both.'

She looked at him as if she thought such thoughtfulness was beyond him and his mouth compressed. He could be thoughtful when the moment called for it.

'And I know what you were referring to.'

She didn't respond but sipped pleasurably at the tea she'd just poured. He watched the way her mouth pursed daintily around the edge of the cup. It hadn't been quite so dainty when it had opened under his six years ago, and no matter how hard he tried he couldn't seem to stop thinking about that.

It had been six years, for heaven's sake. He couldn't even remember the colour of his last lover's hair let alone how she'd tasted, and yet just looking at Lily Wild brought her unique flavour to mind. Her generous curves. Her responsiveness… Ah, the sweetness of a response that had most likely been fuelled by chemical enhancers. Or had it? It was a question that had kept him up late on more than one occasion.

'I feel like I'm on an episode of *This is Your Life.*' She smiled from behind her cup, the incongruous comment thankfully pulling his attention away from her mouth. 'Only the host usually smiles, and

I would have expected at least one or two guests to have turned up by now.'

Tristan scowled—both at the flippant remark and his unquestionable hunger for somebody he didn't even like.

'Okay.' She sighed, completely oblivious to the tumultuous thoughts playing out in his head. 'I'm presuming you don't want my shoe size, so why don't you tell me what happens next and—?'

'No, I don't want your shoe size,' he agreed, cutting her off mid-sentence and leaning back in his chair. Some devil on his shoulder wanted to throw her as off-balance as he felt. 'I already know it. Along with your jeans size, your bra size, and of course what type of panties you like to wear.'

'That's an invasion of privacy,' she snapped.

'So sue me,' he drawled, unaccountably pleased to see her affable expression fade and her eyes flash purple sparks. Her watery attempt at friendship had annoyed him. He didn't want that from her. In fact he didn't want anything at all from her!

Lily pressed her lips together and tried to hold on to her temper. How dared he? Lounging back in his executive chair like King Tut. She took a deep breath and willed herself to remain calm. Polite and aloof…

Just imagine he's a difficult director you have to put up with for a short while. You've done that before.

She was trying to think of some way to regain her equilibrium when Tristan's mobile rang and thankfully he picked it up. He didn't even acknowledge her as he pushed away from his desk and presented her with his back as he walked to stand in the vee of the floor to ceiling windows that partially lined two walls of his corner office.

Lily started reeling through every foul name she could think of to call him, and then her eyes wandered to the view outside his window. London only had a handful of luxury skyscrapers and Tristan owned one of them. It wasn't the tallest, from what she could see, but it was certainly located on prime real estate near the heart of the city. Lily could see Big Ben, Westminster Abbey and the London Eye, and she hadn't had to pay a penny for the privilege.

Without even being aware of it she shifted her gaze from outside the window to the man standing in front of it, legs apart and one hand in his trouser pocket, pulling the fabric of his trousers tight across his taut backside.

Her eyes drifted down over his long legs and up again to the wide sweep of his shoulders, to the ripple of muscle evident beneath his close-fitting shirt. He really was an impressive male and, given his sedentary job, he must work out all the time to stay as fit as he looked.

As if sensing her too-intimate regard, Tristan glanced over his shoulder and pierced her with his green eyes.

The air between them seemed to thicken. Lily's breath caught and her body hummed with a vibrant awareness. Then a dismissive expression flitted across his face, and Lily released a long, steadying breath when he swung his gaze back to the window.

She heard him speaking rapidly to the caller about some EU presentation, effortlessly switching between English and a language she couldn't place. His keen intelligence was evident in the incisive timbre of his voice.

Lily's stomach growled, and she picked up a sandwich from the plate and forced herself to chew it. It was beyond her that she should feel such a strong physical reaction to someone who clearly couldn't stand the sight of her. And it was getting a bit hard to put it down to stress and anxiety. But surely the brain had some input when it came to sexual attraction?

Tristan ended his call, dropped the phone into his pocket and stalked to his desk, gripping the high back of his chair as he studied her with relentless intensity.

'I must say you seem remarkably composed for a woman who's potentially facing at least twenty years in the slammer,' he scorned, leaving Lily stunned by his coldness when minutes earlier there had been such heat.

'I trust the universe will work everything out.' She said, wincing inwardly at her prim tone and refusing to react as he raised a condescending eyebrow.

'The universe? As in the moon, the stars and Mother Earth?'

'No.' Lily tried not to roll her eyes. 'At least not

in the way you mean. The universe is like a force-field—an energy that we create for ourselves and others. Sort of like if we all think positive thoughts then good will always prevail.'

Tristan cocked his head as if he was seriously considering her view, but of course that was a fool's notion. 'Well, I'd say your universe was either out for lunch when you tried walking through Customs today, or it's working perfectly and you're as guilty as hell.'

Lily folded her arms and bit into her top lip.

How was it possible for someone to be so devastatingly attractive one minute and so perversely irritating the next?

'I also have great faith that the authorities know what they're doing,' she said waspishly.

'The authorities want someone to put behind bars.'

Lily angled her chin. 'Are you trying to frighten me?'

'I'm not even sure the Grim Reaper knocking on your door could do that. Perhaps you're not smart enough to see the danger.'

'You're very good with the lofty insults, Lord Garrett, but I believe that right *will* win out in the end.'

Tristan shook his head. 'I'm sure if some of those corpses buried at Tower Hill could speak they'd suggest that was a little whimsical.'

Lily was sure that if some of those corpses could talk they'd tell him they were relatives of hers—and not the blue-blooded ones!

'Are you implying that I'm being unrealistic?'

'Actually, I thought I was doing more than *implying* it.'

Lily sniffed. 'I wouldn't expect someone like you to understand.'

'Someone like me?'

'Someone who thinks everything is either black or white. Someone who requires tangible proof before they'll believe anything.'

'It's called dealing in the real world,' he jibed.

'But sometimes the real world isn't always as it seems.'

Tristan made a scoffing sound. 'I thought I told you I didn't want to hear any of your protestations of innocence.'

Lily's eyes narrowed at his bored tone, and she breathed in deeply through her nose.

Never let 'em know you care, Honeybee.

She exhaled slowly. This would all be a lot easier if he'd just talk to her, instead of snapping off pithy comments here and there.

'And, as *pleasant* as this conversation is,' he continued, 'I have work to do. So I'd prefer you finish your tea and sandwiches over on the sofa.' He sat down and turned to his computer, dismissing her like some servant girl.

Oh, she'd just bet he'd prefer that. And she would have happily done so if he'd been a little nicer, but now...

'Actually, accusations and criticisms do not add

up to a conversation. And would it really hurt you to be a little more civil?' she demanded, throwing the whole idea of polite and aloof out of one of his ultra-clean windows.

'To what end?'

He didn't bother looking up from his computer screen and that incensed her. 'To…to… I don't know. Just to be *nice*.'

'I don't do nice.'

Lily nearly laughed.

As if she hadn't worked that one out for herself! 'You know, for someone whose job it is to communicate with others you're not very good at it.'

That got his attention. 'My job is about justice, not communication. And you better be careful because I'm really good at it.'

Lily shook her head. The man needed to learn some home truths. 'You might be hot stuff in the courtroom, Lord Garrett, but personally you're an avoider. You'd rather shut me up than try to have a constructive conversation with me.'

'That's because I don't *want* to have a conversation with you—constructive or otherwise.'

Lily raised her eyebrows. 'That's a fine way to solve a problem.'

'I don't have… No—wait.' He tapped his pen impatiently on his desk. 'I *do* have a problem. She's blonde, five-foot-ten and won't stop jabbering on at me as if I care.'

Lily's mouth gaped, and she stuck her tongue

against the back of her front teeth to prevent herself from telling him just what she thought of his rude comments and hurtful attitude.

'You really think you've got me all sussed out, don't you, Tristan?' Her voice was husky with raw emotion. 'I'm just some no-good dumb celebrity who takes drugs and uses the casting couch to get her roles as far as you're concerned.'

'Well, not if you're screwing the dolly boy. I can't imagine *he* can win you too many roles.' He leaned back in his chair and folded his arms behind his head.

Arrogant jerk.

Lily narrowed her eyes and stabbed her finger in his direction. 'You might have some two-bit report on your desk, but let me tell you—you know nothing about me. Absolutely nothing.'

'I know all I need to know,' he confirmed.

Lily shook her head. She was wasting her breath trying to talk to him. He'd made up his mind about her a long time ago and there was nothing she could do to sway it. In fact, when the police found out who the real drug smuggler was he'd probably accuse her of sleeping with the whole police force to get the result.

She gave a slight shake of her head. When she'd left England six years ago she'd instigated a policy never to rise to people's bad opinion of her again, but for some reason she couldn't seem to help herself with Tristan. For some reason his condescending attitude hurt more than everybody else's put together—and she hated that.

Lily folded her arms across her chest and decided to give up all attempts to change his opinion. Let him think what he wanted.

'You know it's a good thing you're not my lawyer because I'd fire you.'

'Fire me?' He gave a harsh burst of laughter. 'Sweetheart, I wouldn't touch this case if it came gold-plated.' He sat straighter and looked down his aristocratic nose at her. 'Because I know what you are, Honey Blossom Lily Wild—or have you conveniently forgotten what happened at Jordana's eighteenth?'

Lily stiffened at the ominously quiet question. Here was the basis of his true hatred of her. The presumed ruination of his little sister because of her association with big, bad Lily Wild. He'd judged her on circumstantial evidence at least twice before, and she hated that he had never once given her the benefit of the doubt.

'You know—you know,' she spat, ignoring the inner voice that told her to calm down. 'I could make a movie about what you *don't* know, you ignorant jerk, and it would be an instant classic.'

'Ignorant jerk?'

That seemed to rile him, and it startled her when his chair shot back, nearly tipping over with the force of his movement. He circled his desk, a predatory in-tent in every silent step, and Lily's heart bumped behind her ribs. She didn't think he'd hurt her, but still, the instinct to run was nearly overwhelming.

He stopped just in front of her, his hands balled on his hips, his green eyes ablaze with suppressed emotion.

'Let's see,' he snarled, leaning over her and caging her in with his hands on the armrests of her chair. 'You tried to hide a joint under my sister's mattress when you were fourteen, you took her to sleazy parties in the city—*underage*—you caused an outrageous scandal the night of her eighteenth, snorting cocaine from the glass front of my father's *seven-hundred-year-old* Giotto painting, and today you cart a truckload of charlie and disco biscuits into Heathrow.' He leaned in closer. The pronounced muscles in his forearms bunched. 'Tell me, Honey, how am I doing so far with what I *don't* know about you?'

Lily felt the back of the chair hard against her spine and ran her tongue over her dry lips. She could explain every one of those things—but he wasn't looking for an explanation, and frankly she was getting so sick of his rudeness she almost wanted him to dig a hole so she could bury him in it.

She remained tight-lipped, and his mocking expression said it all.

'What? No comment all of a sudden? No further explanation as to why I walked into my father's study and found a group of wasted idiots—my sister being one of them—and you leaning over the desk holding a rolled fifty-pound note, with some Armani-clad idiot standing behind you like he was getting ready to take you? What a surprise.'

Lily blushed profusely at his bluntness. That wasn't how it had been at all—but had it really looked like that? And how could he think she'd even been interested in that guy after the kisses they had shared?

'For heaven's sake, why would I kiss you if I—? Oh.' She stopped abruptly and nodded. 'You think I just went from you to him. Hence the cheap slut reference.' She shook her head as if she was truly stupid. 'Sorry, I'm a slow learner. Maybe you can add dumb blonde to my list of credentials? That's if you haven't done it already, of course.'

Tristan moved as quickly as a striking snake and reached down to pull her to her feet. 'Stop. Trying. To. Garner. My. Sympathies. You took a chance. It didn't come off. Now, deal with it.'

Lily tried to pull her hands free, and then stopped when she realised it was a futile waste of energy. Her eyes blazed into his. 'I don't know what ever made me think I could reason with you,' she bit out, adrenaline coursing through her veins. 'You know what? Go to hell. All you do is judge me and I've had it. You've never wanted the truth where I'm concerned and—oof!'

The air left her body as Tristan pulled her hard up against him and covered her mouth with his own. She tasted anger and frustration—and something else.

Something that called to her. Something that left her mind reeling. After a token struggle she felt her resistance ebb away. Her brain simply shut down, leaving her body and her heart firmly in charge, and both, it seemed, craved his touch more than air.

Tristan knew it was a mistake as soon as he did it— but, seriously, just how much self-control did she think he possessed? Did she never give up? Standing there, glorious in her anger, her eyes sparkling like cabochon amethysts.

She shoved against him and tried to twist her mouth away, but Tristan wound her ponytail around his fist and held her head fast. Some distant part of his brain tried reminding him that he didn't behave like this. That he didn't shut women up with his mouth like some Neolithic cave dweller.

But it was too late. He'd been hungry for the taste of her all day, and something far more primitive than logic and civility was riding him now.

She moaned, her hands pushing against his shoulders, and he immediately gentled the pressure of his mouth. A voice in his head was telling him to stop. That now he was behaving like a jerk. That he hated this woman whose mouth felt like hot velvet under his.

She represented everything wrong with mankind. She took drugs, she partied hard, she was self-centered, self-absorbed—like his mother. Just when he might have had a chance of pulling away her finger-nails curled into his shoulders, no longer pushing him away but drawing him closer, and he was lost.

He eased the hand in her hair and pressed his other one to her lower back, to bring her into firmer contact with his body, and delighted in her responsive quiver.

Right now he didn't give a damn about parties and drugs. Right now he was satisfying an urge that had started six years ago and got a whole lot worse today. He felt a groan rise up from his chest as her lips moved almost shyly beneath his. He wanted her. Hell, his body was aching with it. And he knew by the way her fingers clutched at his shirt that she felt the feral chemistry between them as intensely as he did.

He softened his lips even more and felt hers cling.

'Open your mouth, Honey,' he urged. 'I need to taste you.'

She obeyed instantly, and his tongue slid home and drank from her as if she was the finest wine. Only she tasted better. Sweeter than he remembered. He nearly expired at the shocking pleasure that jack-knifed through his body. She was like ambrosia to his senses, and he was once again reminded how men could start wars over a woman. And then he lost the ability to think at all as her tongue snuck into his mouth and she raised herself onto her toes to deepen the contact between them.

It was all the encouragement Tristan needed, and

he widened his stance to take more of her weight, burning up when she rubbed her full breasts against his chest. Her soft, breathy whimpers incited him never to stop this crazy dance. His hands were unsteady as they skimmed down her torso, skating over her breasts and pulling her restless hips more firmly against his almost painful arousal.

She gasped and pressed even closer, buried her hands in his over-long hair.

Tristan couldn't contain another groan, and his hands rose up to push her cumbersome cardigan aside so that he could palm her breasts with both hands. She arched into him and his thumbs flicked over her peaked nipples. His senses revelled in her soft cries of pleasure. His lips drifted down over her neck as he dragged oxygen into his starved lungs, and he slid one hand down to delve underneath the elastic waistband of her tight leggings to cup her bottom. Her skin felt gloriously smooth and hot, and there was no thought of stopping now. He'd wanted this for too long, and he knew when he touched between her legs she'd be wet and wanting...

The strident buzz of his intercom resounded through the room like a death knell, and Tristan sprang back from Lily as if he'd been kicked.

'Tristan, I know you said no interruptions, but Jordana is on line one and threatening legal action if you don't take her call.' His secretary's humorous voice rang out clear, despite the blood roaring in his ears.

Hell. Everyone was a comedian all of a sudden.

'Tristan?'

'Fine,' he snapped. 'Tell her I'll be a minute.'

He watched Lily blink a couple of times, her hands on her heaving chest, her eyes hidden as she contemplated the foot of black carpet between them as if it was a seething pit of snakes. Her lips were deeply pink and swollen from his kisses.

He shook his head at his own stupidity.

He wasn't some hotheaded youth at the mercy of his untried hormones. What had he been thinking?

He noted the rise of hot colour that started at her neck and swept into her face. He didn't know if it was from embarrassment or desire.

'Hell,' he seethed, stalking back round to his side of the desk, raking his fingers through his hair. He willed his body to calm down. 'We are *not* going to do this. You are *not* going to look at me with that come-hither sexiness. You want to know what happens next? I'll tell you. You sit over there on that sofa and you don't move. You don't talk and you don't whine. The only thing you're allowed to do without me is go to the bathroom, and if I think you're up to no good in there you'll lose that privilege as well. Is that clear enough for you?'

'Crystal,' she snapped, straightening her clothing and pulling her cardigan tightly around her body.

She touched her tongue to her lips and another shaft of desire shot into his aching groin. Then she raised her chin and looked at him with over-bright eyes, and once again he felt like the jerk she'd called him earlier.

'You know,' she began softly, 'Jordana thinks you're one of the good guys. Boy, does she have *that* wrong.'

CHAPTER SIX

TRISTAN sat opposite his sister at one of London's most exclusive eateries and tried not to brood over Lily's earlier comment. Because Jordana was right, damn it. He *was* one of the good guys, and he didn't know why he was letting the two-bit actress beside him, laughing over Oliver's unfunny jokes, make him question that.

Maybe because he'd kissed her the way a man kissed a woman he planned to sleep with and then blamed her for it. As if this maddening desire he felt for her was a deliberate spell she had cast over him... Which, come to think of it, was a much better explanation than the alternative—that he just couldn't keep his hands off her.

Which was not the case at all. What had happened in his office earlier was the result of extreme stress boiling over. Nothing more, nothing less.

Tristan prided himself on his emotional objectivity when it came to the fairer sex, and really this constant analysis of what had happened earlier was ludicrous. Yes, he was a man who liked his '*i*'s' dotted and his '*t*'s' crossed, but Lily was just an anomaly. An outlier on an otherwise predictable curve.

So what if his reaction to her was at the extreme end of the scale? It happened. Not often to *him* before, granted, but…once she was gone and his world had returned to normal he'd forget about her—as he had done the last time.

As he had done every other woman who had graced his bed.

Only Lily hadn't graced his bed, and maybe that went some way to explaining his almost obsessive thoughts about her. He'd never had her. Had, in fact, made her off-limits to himself. And he wanted her. No point denying the obvious. Maybe if he had her— *no!* Forget it. Not going to happen.

But that didn't change the fact that now that his ferocious anger at being caught up in her situation had abated, and now he'd had a chance to observe her with Oliver and his sister all night, he had to admit he was starting to question his earlier assessment of her.

There was something so earthy and genuine about her. Something so lacking in artifice. He'd noticed it when she had engaged in a conversation with his PA and three of his paralegal secretaries.

She hadn't tried to brush them off, or spoken down to them. She'd been warm and friendly and called them by name. Something he would not have expected a drug-addicted diva to remember, let alone do.

He couldn't comprehend that he might have been

wrong about her—but nor could he ignore the sixth sense that told him that something didn't add up.

Especially since the police believed that the haul found in Lily's bag, although small, had been intended for resale purposes. Lily just didn't strike him as the type who worked for a drug cartel, and nor did she appear to need money. Which left the possibility that she was innocent, had been framed, or had been an unknowing drug mule.

Or she'd brought the drugs in for a lover.

In his business Tristan had come across people who did far worse things for love, and he told himself the only reason he cared about this possibility was because he felt sorry for her. If she was so in love with some jerk she'd committed a crime for him she would definitely do jail-time. Lots of jail-time.

As if all that wasn't bad enough, the langoustines poached in miso—Élan's signature dish, which he had enjoyed many times before—had failed to get the taste of her out of his mouth. And that was just damned annoying.

Lily shifted on the black leather bench seat beside him and for the millionth time he wished she'd just sit still. They had been given a corner booth, overlooking Hyde Park, and whenever she so much as blinked, or turned to take in the view, his mind thought it was a good idea to let him know about it.

He glanced around at the *über*-modern, low-lit interior and recognised some of the more celebrated restaurant clientele, who all seemed to be having a better time of it than him. Laughter and perfume wafted through the air, along with the sound of flatware on Limoges china, but none of it could distract him from his unhealthy awareness of her.

He reached for his glass and took a long pull of classic 1956 Mouton Rothschild Medoc, forcing his attention from the spoon Lily was trying to lick the last morsel of ice cream from, as if it was thousand-pound-an-ounce caviar, and back to Oliver's discourse about his barbaric Scottish ancestors and some battle he'd no doubt claim they had won against the English.

God, his friend could talk. Had he known that about him?

Lily leaned forward and laughed, and Tristan refused to look at the way her low-cut silk blouse dipped invitingly, wondering where her tent-like cardigan had disappeared to.

When they had arrived at Jordana's prior to dinner the two girls had cried and hugged for an eternity. Then Jordana had whisked Lily away to shower and change, berating him for not thinking of it himself. Tristan hadn't told her that the last thing he needed was to have Lily Wild naked in his shower!

Now she was dressed in a red gypsy blouse, fitted denims and ankle boots, all provided by his sister. Her hair was brushed and fell in shiny waves down her back and she'd put on a bra. Pink. Demi-cup. Though he'd be a lot happier not knowing that. Because she had fabulous breasts and he couldn't help wondering what they would look like naked.

'It was love at first sight.'

Jordana's words sounded overly loud to his ears, and brought his awareness sharply back to the conversation.

What was?

Tristan looked at his sister, who was thankfully gazing at her fiancé and not at him, and released a breath he hadn't even realised he was holding.

'That's rubbish,' Oliver grouched. 'It took a month of haranguing you to help me find the perfect anniversary present for my parents before you even agreed to a real date.'

'I wasn't talking about me!' Jordana giggled pointedly, and then squealed when Oliver grabbed her leg under the table.

Lily laughed at their antics—a soft, musical sound that curled through Tristan's abdomen like a witch's spell.

'Steady on,' he said, as much to himself as to Oliver. 'She's still my baby sister, you know.'

'Stop your whining, you great plonker,' Oliver retorted. 'You're just jealous because you can't find someone who'll have you.'

'Ah, but haven't you heard, my good friend?' Tristan drawled. 'A man doesn't know what real happiness is until he's married. And by then it's too late!'

Jordana pulled a face. 'Oh, ha-ha. You'll fall in love one day. Once you get your head out of those legal bibles and stop dating women who are entirely unsuitable.'

'That swimwear model didn't look too unsuitable to me.' Oliver grinned.

'That swimwear model looked like a bobby pin.' Jordana said archly. 'Or should I say *booby* pin?'

'Lady Sutton, then?' Oliver offered.

'Hmmm, right pedigree, but—'

'I *am* still here, you know,' Tristan grumbled, 'and I'll thank you both for staying out of my personal affairs. There's nothing worse than two people who think love conquers all trying to talk perfectly happy singles into jumping off the same cliff.'

Not to mention the fact that he had no plans to relinquish his freedom to such a fickle and painful emotion as love.

But that reminded him that now would be a good time to find out who Lily could be so in love with she'd risk everything to please him.

And he had a right to know. He'd stuck his neck out for her, and he'd be damned if he'd risk getting it cut off because she'd done some idiot's bidding.

'What about you, Lily? Ever been in love?' he asked, smiling benignly as she shot him a look that would have felled a tree.

Now, what on earth had made Tristan ask her that? He'd ignored her all night, and when he did speak to her it was to ask something she had no intention of answering. Not seriously anyway...

'Oh, gosh, how long have you got?' Lily jested lightly, trying to think of a feasible way to change the subject. She'd rather talk about money than love!

'As long as it takes,' Tristan replied amiably.

She cast him a frosty look and murmured her thanks as a waiter discreetly refilled her water glass just before she picked it up.

Tristan scowled at him, but Lily appreciated his attentiveness. As she did the 'no cameras' policy the restaurant insisted on. No doubt the main reason the place was so well-attended by the super rich. Although, as to that, this restaurant exuded a class all of its own.

Eating out had been the last thing Lily had felt like doing, especially after the incident in Tristan's office, but she'd have done anything not to be alone with him. Which she would be once they left the restaurant.

And now he wanted to discuss her love-life as if they were best friends!

She didn't think so.

There was no way she would tell him that, yes, she had thought herself silly enough to be in love once.

With *him*!

Especially not when she had returned those kisses in his office a few hours earlier as if she still *was* in love with him. Unbelievably, her body had gone off on a tangent completely at odds with her mind, and she was still shocked by her behaviour.

And his.

Although she shouldn't be. Tristan had been angry and had shut her up in the most primitive way possible. It didn't make it right—in fact it was downright wrong—but then so had been her response. She should have slapped him, not kissed him back. All she'd done was confirm his view that she was easy. A view she already knew would be impossible to reverse, so why even try? It wasn't as if he would believe the truth anyway.

'Well, let's see...' Lily paused, avoiding Jordana's interested gaze and counting on her fingers. 'First there was Clem Watkins, and then Joel Meaghan. Then—'

'Joel Major, you mean? And Clem? The guy from the gym squad?' Jordana scoffed. 'He had a nose that looked like he'd gone ten rounds with a hockey stick and he thought the ozone layer was a computer game.'

Lily pasted on a smile. 'He had good teeth, and he realised his mistake about the ozone layer almost straight away.'

'After everyone laughed. How could you have been in love with them? You didn't date either one.'

And that, Lily thought as she tried to ignore Jordana's frowning visage, was one of the problems with ad-libbing. Or telling white lies. You made mistakes.

Like forgetting that your closest friend was also at the dinner table and knew almost all of your teenage secrets.

'I'm not interested in your high-school dalliances,

Lily.' Tristan cut in scathingly, his voice rising over the sounds of laughter in the background. 'I do want to get home tonight. Let's talk about *men* you've been in love with.'

Ha!

'Let's not,' Lily said, dismissing him with one of her enigmatic smiles. 'You'd be bored silly.'

'Humour me,' he insisted, his tone intimate as he shifted his hand along the back of the velvet seat. 'Who's the current love of your life?'

His thumb grazed one of her shoulderblades and the heat of his touch burned through her thin blouse like dry ice.

Lily jerked forward and pretended she had been about to place her water glass back on the table.

He had done that deliberately, and if she hadn't agreed to put on a united front for Jordana and Oliver she'd happily tell him where to go.

Looking at the sexy little smile curving his lips, she knew he knew it. Which only fuelled her ire. If he thought he had the upper hand in this situation he had another thing coming.

'Oh, don't be silly,' she cooed, reaching across and placing her hand a little too high on his thigh, and patting him as one might a family pet. 'You already know everything there is to know about me. Remember?'

She felt a spurt of pleasure when Tristan looked taken aback by her action.

'I thought it was your contention that I didn't?'

He replied lazily, smiling a devil's smile and clamping his larger hand over hers, effectively imprisoning her palm against his muscular thigh. 'I've always believed it's better to go directly to the source when you want to find something out.'

Lily's smile froze as his steely thigh muscles contracted beneath her palm. Her fingernails automatically curled into his trousers and she gave serious consideration to piercing through the heavy fabric to the flesh beneath.

Heat surged through her body as he squeezed her hand and locked his darkly amused eyes with hers. Lily shifted her gaze to the twinkling lights of the park through the unadorned windows before managing to recover her equilibrium enough to flick her dismissive gaze back over him.

'How very open-minded of you,' she purred pointedly, digging her nails into his thigh once more before dragging her hand away.

Lily had wanted to put Tristan in his place, but instead he threw his head back and laughed—a delightfully masculine sound that was like fingernails down a chalkboard to her highly strung emotions.

She could see Jordana and Oliver looking perplexed, and then Tristan smiled at her. 'That's just the kind of guy I am,' he said, picking up his wine glass and holding her gaze as he stroked his thumb over the stem.

'I take it that was an in-joke?' Jordana offered, jolting Lily's attention away from Tristan.

'I don't know.' Lily sniffed. 'I didn't find it funny at all.'

'Well, regardless, now I'm even more confused.' Jordana tilted her head. 'Are you seeing someone, Lil, or not?'

Lily saw the open curiosity in her friend's face and wished she could rewind the last few minutes—because Jordana was far too nosy and would no doubt start hassling her about how hard she worked and how she needed to get out more.

'No.' She sighed, and then, feeling herself observed by Tristan's sceptical gaze, added, 'No one of any importance, that is.'

Let him make of that what he would!

'Well, good,' Jordana surprised her by saying. 'Because like Tristan, you've gone for completely the wrong partners so far. But—' she raised her index finger as Lily was about to intercede '—as you're my best friend I've decided to help you out.'

'How?' There was nothing scarier than Jordana on a love mission.

'Ah, not telling. Let's just say I have a little surprise for you during the wedding celebrations.' Jordana cast Oliver a conspiratorial glance from behind her crystal wine glass.

Lily didn't even try to smile.

'Jordana, what are you up to?'

'Now, don't be like that,' Jordana admonished her. 'I know how hard you've worked the past couple of years and it's time you cut loose a little bit. Look around, Lil.' She waved her glass towards the row of white tabletops. 'Have some fun, like your peers.'

Lily gave her friend what she hoped was a good-natured grimace. Jordana was sounding more and more like her old therapist, and that was just plain scary. 'Jordana, you're starting to scare me, and—much as I hate to agree with Tristan—I think you're so loved-up at the minute you're blinkered. I'm very happy as I am. I don't want a relationship. I like being single.'

'I'm just loading the gun, Lil, you don't have to fire the bullets,' Jordana returned innocently. 'Now, how about a pot of tea to finish off?'

'We really should be going,' Tristan said. 'Lily's tired.'

Lily looked at him, surprised he'd noticed. She *was* tired, but she'd do anything to prolong the time before being alone with him.

'No, I'm not.' She smiled brightly. 'And I never finish a meal without a cup of peppermint tea.'

'I'll have one too,' Jordana said.

Tristan and Oliver both raised their hands to signal the waiter at the same time, and Lily couldn't help laughing. Clearly Jordana had found herself an alpha male top dog to stand up to her overbearing brother.

The waiter took their order and Lily excused herself to use the bathroom.

Tristan frowned at her as she stood up, and she knew exactly what he was thinking. 'Be a dear and mind my handbag, would you?' she said to him, tilting the smaller satchel she had brought along in place of her tote precariously towards him and enjoying the way his eyes flared at her provocative move.

Serve him right for asking her such a personal question before, and trapping her hand against his thigh.

'Lily! Hi.'

Lily looked up into the mirror above the handbasin into the gorgeous face of a previous co-star she had shot a film with two years ago.

'I thought it was you. Summer Berkley—we worked together on *Honeymooner.*'

'Yes, I remember.' Lily wiped her hands.

Summer was a quintessential LA actress, with the tan, the boobs, no hips whatsoever and the hair just so. But she had a good heart, and a genuine talent which would eventually take her further than all the rest combined.

They swapped stories for a few minutes, and when Lily couldn't stall in the bathroom any more without drawing attention to the fact that she was doing so, she reluctantly preceded Summer into the dimly lit corridor—and almost straight into Tristan, leaning indolently against the opposite wall, arms folded, legs crossed at the ankles.

'Oh, *hello*,' Summer breathed behind her, and Lily mentally rolled her eyes. 'Are you waiting for us?'

'In a manner of speaking.' Tristan smiled at the redheaded Summer with bemused interest.

Lily decided there was no way she was standing around to watch Tristan hit on another woman, but when she moved to sidestep him he deliberately snagged his hand around her waist to waylay her.

Lily stiffened, and couldn't miss Summer's disappointed pout before she strutted suggestively past Tristan, who looked designer casual with the top buttons of his shirt undone and a five o'clock shadow darkening his chiselled jaw.

'I'm sorry, Lord Garrett. Did I take more than my allotted thirty seconds?' Lily murmured, stepping away from his touch.

Tristan let her go and held up his mobile phone. 'I had to take a call. But, yes, as a matter of fact, you did. And deliberately, I have no doubt.'

'Now, why would I do that?'

'Oh, I don't know.' His smile didn't reach his eyes. 'Because you like bugging me?'

'Hardly,' Lily denied, looking down her nose at him. 'Do you mind?' She looked pointedly towards the restaurant's dining room.

'Why don't you want me to know who your current lover is?' he asked.

Lily stared at the stubble on his chin and wondered absurdly if it was hard or soft. 'If I ignore you will you go away?' she queried hopefully.

'Nope.'

She sighed. 'How about because it's none of your business, then?'

'Is he famous?'

'No.'

She had to step closer to Tristan to allow two women to walk past, but quickly stepped back again.

'Married?'

'No!'

'Do I know him?'

Lily let out a breath. She couldn't understand why he was pushing this. He was starting to sound like a jealous beau. But that was ridiculous. He didn't even *like* her, did he?

'I don't see that it's any of your business,' she said again with icy politeness, folding her hands across her chest.

'Unfortunately for you everything about you right now is very much my business.'

Lily shook her head. 'I don't see how. You're not my lawyer, and the question is irrele—'

She broke off with a squeak as Tristan grabbed her elbow again, to avoid more diners heading to the bathroom and marched her around a short corner, stopping in front of a closed door.

They were close enough now that Lily could feel heat—and anger—emanating from his muscular frame.

'If you brought those drugs into the country for someone else,' he began scathingly, 'and you get approached by the moron while you're in my custody I could be implicated. Not only could my reputation and legal practice go down the drain but, depending on how it played out, I could be charged along with you.' His voice never lost its tenor, and the message was clear. 'So, whether you think my questions are relevant or not is completely *irrelevant* to me.'

Lily's heart beat heavily in her chest. So that was what was behind his earlier probing. She had been right. He wasn't interested in her as a person. She hated the fact that for a brief moment she had toyed with the idea that he might actually like her. Talk about living in a dream world.

She swallowed, not wanting to dwell on the way that made her feel—because she couldn't—wouldn't—continue to be disappointed by his low opinion of her.

She looked furtively around the small space and realised she was trapped between some sort of cupboard and Tristan and would need to push past him to return to the dining room.

For a minute she considered ignoring him, but she knew how well that would go down. And nobody had ever benefited from pulling a tiger's tail that she knew of…

'I wasn't anyone's drug mule and I don't know who the drugs belong to or how they ended up in my bag. And, contrary to *popular* belief, I don't have a lover right now. Sorry to disappoint you on that score.'

His brooding gaze held hers, and Lily resisted the urge to slick her tongue across her lips. He looked annoyed and intimidating, and a lot like he had when he'd thrown her out of his family home six years ago.

'What happened in my father's study six years

ago?' he asked suddenly, and Lily wondered if maybe he really was a mind reader!

'You threw me out of your home and told me not to contact Jo again,' she said immediately.

'Which you ignored.'

Her eyes widened. 'Did you really expect me to cut myself off from her?'

His lips curved up slightly, as if he found the question amusing, but his eyes remained hard. 'Of course I expected it. But there's nothing I can do about that now. And that's not what I was asking about and you know it.'

If he was asking about the private party he had interrupted at Jo's eighteenth that was his problem. If Jordana hadn't already told him that *she* had instigated the party then Lily wouldn't do it either. It wouldn't serve any purpose but to make him think poorly of Jo, and Lily had no intention of ruining relations between them so close to the wedding by being some sort of tattle-tale after the event.

'I see no point in rehashing the past,' she said.

'Well, that's too bad, because I do.'

Lily unconsciously squared her shoulders. 'Actually, it's too bad for you, because I don't.'

Tristan's eyes narrowed dangerously. 'You were keen enough to talk earlier.'

'And you pointed out what a terrible idea that was, and now I'm agreeing with you.'

'Careful, Lily. That's twice you've agreed with me... Don't want to make a habit of it.'

Lily leaned forward and balled her hands on her hips. 'Well, here's something else I agree with you about—we need to set some ground rules before we go any further, and your macho "I'm in charge" routine just isn't going to cut it. Especially in public.'

'Really?'

'Yes, really.' Lily angled her chin up, ignoring the mocking glint in his eyes. 'And the first rule is that what happened back in your office is never to be repeated.'

'Now, how did I know you were going to say that?' he murmured silkily.

'I don't know. Putting that off-the-scale IQ of yours to good use for once?' she quipped, a sense of her own control making her reckless.

'Don't pretend you didn't want it,' he grated. 'You've been eating me up with your eyes ever since I picked you up today.'

'Oh!' Lily forgot about the fact that they were in a public space. 'You are something else!'

'So I've been told.'

'I just bet you have. You have quite the reputation as a ladies' man, but if you think I want to join their lowly ranks you can think again.'

'That's not how you played it six years ago,' he sneered.

'Six years ago I was too young to know any better—and don't forget I was high as a kite,' she lied. Why not *really* play up to his nasty opinion of her? Answering honestly before hadn't done much to change his opinion of her.

'Well, that might be.' His eyes flashed in response to her taunt. 'But you weren't high back in my office, and the way you tried to crawl up my body you wouldn't have stopped until I was deep inside you and you were completely sated.'

Lily gasped. His words conjured up a sensual image that caused her pelvis to clench alarmingly. 'You're delusional if you think that,' Lily spat breathlessly.

The cupboard's doorknob poked into her back as she instinctively moved back when Tristan closed the small space between them.

His eyes glittered dangerously into hers. 'A challenge, Honey?'

'No!'

'Oh, yes.'

He placed a hand either side of her head and leaned in, his mouth so close she could feel his warm breath on her lips, smell the coffee and wine he'd consumed.

Lily's heart sounded as loud as a road train in her ears, and her pelvis continued to clench in wicked anticipation of his kiss. Try as she might, she couldn't seem to find the will to resist his animal magnetism that was pulling her under.

Tristan's gaze held hers for a lifetime. 'Oh, yes,' he whispered again. 'Definitely a challenge.' He straightened away from her and dropped his arms, his expression closed. 'But, as gorgeous as you undoubtedly are, I'm not interested—so go play your games somewhere else.'

CHAPTER SEVEN

THE ride to Tristan's home was tense, to say the least. Lily was still fuming over the humiliation of nearly embarrassing herself before, when she had almost reached up and pulled Tristan's taunting mouth to hers. Something she hadn't even been aware she was about to do until he'd pulled back.

Until *he'd* pulled back.

She swallowed a moan of distress and watched one neon sign become another as Tristan steered his silver Mercedes through the streets from Park Lane to Hampstead Heath—one of London's most prestigious addresses.

How dared he tell her that he wasn't interested in her? As if she would care! How about the fact that *she* wasn't interested in *him*?

And he'd certainly been a little more than interested back in his office. Interested in sex, anyway. Not that she would have let it get that far. But deep down she knew what he was trying to say. She wasn't his type. He thought her attractive, but nothing more.

Frank Murphy, her stepfather, had warned her

about men like Tristan. 'They'll take one look at that face and figure and, believe me, they won't care about your personality. You give them what they want and you'll get a reputation for being easy.' *Like your mother.* The unspoken words had hung between them and Lily shifted uncomfortably at the memory.

Her mother had been ruled by her desires. Or, more specifically, her desire for Johnny Wild, but Lily wasn't like that. Which was one of the reasons she resented this attraction she still felt for Tristan. She'd sworn never to fall for an unattainable man, and here she was all but salivating over one.

Dammit, Tristan was right. She had wanted him earlier in his office. Had, in fact, been completely enthralled by the sensations and emotions his touch had evoked.

The memory made her cheeks heat with shame. Hadn't she learned anything from his first rejection of her? Was she just a glutton for punishment?

Lily sighed and leaned her head back against the butter-soft leather seat, wishing she hadn't decided to come back to England after all this time. She should never have told Jordana she could make her wedding. Would be *in* her wedding!

It seemed that the stars had aligned and no matter which way she looked she was being sent a message that she wasn't as ready to come home as she had thought. And maybe she never would be.

Thankfully her morose thoughts halted when Tristan's powerful car pulled up and waited for the ten-metre-high wrought-iron gates to open. Lily glanced at the towering stone mansion softly lit by discreet exterior lights that made it seem as if it touched the skyline.

The car inched forward and down into an underground car park that held a motorbike, a four-wheel drive, and a gleaming red sports car.

A sense of entrapment suffused her, and Lily felt so tense she jumped out of the car before it had come to a complete stop. Then wished she hadn't as she swayed and had to grab hold of the roof to steady herself.

Tristan's mouth tightened, but he didn't say anything as she followed him to a lift.

A *lift*!

'The house belonged to an elderly couple before I bought it,' he said, noticing her surprised reaction.

Lily didn't respond; emotional exhaustion and jet lag were weighing her down as effectively as a giant bag of sand. She calculated that it was about 5:00 a.m. in Bangkok, which meant that she'd been up all night, and the effort it took to work that out made her nearly trip over her own feet when the lift doors opened.

Tristan cursed and reached for her, and cursed again when she stumbled trying to avoid him.

'Don't be a fool,' he ground out as she wrenched her elbow out of his reach.

'I don't want you touching me,' she snapped, wedging herself into the far corner of the panelled lift and staring at his shoes.

'Fine—fall over, then,' he mocked, moving to the opposite side of the small space.

Tristan had briefly considered arguing with her, but if she wanted to deny the sexual chemistry between them then that was her prerogative. He should probably take a leaf out of her book and do the same thing. It had been silly, goading her in the restaurant, rising to her challenge. A challenge, he'd sensed from her awkwardness afterwards, that had been more innocent than intentional.

And maybe he'd have more success ignoring the chemistry between them if she'd stop flinching every time he came within spitting distance of her? Because that just made a primitive part of him want to pursue her even more.

'You need to stop doing that,' he said.

She raised her eyes from his feet all the way up his body and looked at him from under pitch-black lashes. 'Breathing?' she quipped, folding her arms across her chest as he mimicked her leisurely scrutiny.

He barely resisted the urge to smile. *Yeah, that would help.*

She glanced away and worried her top lip and he wished she'd stop doing that as well.

The lift doors opened and Tristan strode out and dumped his keys on the small hallway table, walking through the vast foyer and up the marble stair-case. He noticed her glance around at the pristine surroundings and the priceless artwork on the walls as she trailed behind.

His home was modern and elegant, with eclectic pieces he'd picked up from his travels here and there, and he wondered what she thought of it. And then wondered why he cared.

He stopped outside the room he'd asked his house-keeper to allocate to her. 'This is your room. Mine's at the end of the hall.'

He opened the door and stood back to let her pre-cede him inside. When her scent hit him between the eyes he steeled himself against what he was about to do.

'As you can see, your suitcases are already in-side the dressing room and the *en suite* bathroom is through there.' He flicked open another door and hit the light switch. 'My housekeeper was instructed to make the room ready, so you should have everything you need.'

She didn't say anything, just stood beside the silk-covered queen-sized bed clutching her bag.

'I'll need to see the bag before I go,' he said evenly.

'What for?' She snapped her eyes to his.

Because after she had spent so long in the bath-room at the restaurant with that redhead with the fake lips he had wondered if she hadn't slipped Lily a little something. Of course Lily might have already taken it, but he hadn't seen any evidence of that when he'd backed her up against the cupboard in the restaurant. All he'd seen then was a heady desire that matched his own.

He knew the chances of the woman giving Lily something were slim to none, but with a Scotland Yard detective due to interview her in the morning he wasn't prepared to take that chance.

'The bag.'

She narrowed her eyes. 'You already know what's in it. Remember?'

'That was before you visited with your friend in the restaurant bathroom.'

'Oh, come on. It's not like I planned to run into her.' Lily's tone was incredulous.

Tristan held out his hand and Lily lobbed her bag at him as if it was a missile. 'Have it—and good luck to you.'

Tristan walked closer to her and upended the contents onto the bed. There wasn't much to see but cosmetics and a purse. He checked the purse and then dropped it back on the bed.

'Now you.'

She didn't move, and he clenched his jaw when he saw understanding dawn across her stunning face.

'Tell me you're kidding.'

He sincerely wished he could. 'The way I see it we can do this one of two ways. Either I search you or you strip.'

She made a small sound and then slapped her hands on her hips. Her eyes, when they met his, were glacial. 'Is this how you get your kicks? Trying to frighten innocent women into doing what you want?'

'I didn't ask for this,' he grated, his eyes drawn to the little gap at the centre of her blouse where the red ribbon tied in a bow. 'But it's my house. My rules. So—arms out.'

He stepped towards her and she stepped backwards—and came up against the bedside table.

Her gaze flitted between him and the bedroom door, as if she was contemplating making a run for it. 'I'm clean. I promise you I am.'

'Don't make this harder than it has to be.' He stopped just in front of her.

The colour was high on her cheekbones and the pulse-point in her neck looked as if it was trying to break free. Just when he thought he'd have to consider force she surprised him by suddenly opening her arms wide.

'Go ahead. You don't scare me.'

Tristan stepped forward. Impudent witch. He might be as hard as stone at the thought of touching her but he actually resented having to touch her like this. No matter how much he tried to deny it to himself, he knew that he would much prefer her willing and wanting. And he'd lied to her before. He *was* interested. Too interested.

Wanting to get this over with as quickly as possible Tristan circled her tiny wrists and ran both his hands up the long sleeves of her blouse at the same time.

'My stepfather warned me about men like you,' she said, her voice a breathy caress in the otherwise silent room.

'Is that right?' His hands rounded her shoulders and then ran lightly under the heavy cascade of her hair and across her back. He felt her shiver and swallowed hard.

'That's right—*oh*!' She gasped as his hands skimmed around her ribcage and rose to cup her breasts. Her nipples peaked against his palms and made it nearly impossible for him to leave that tiny bow done up.

'Keep talking,' he growled, his hands skimming back down over her torso. It was easier to ignore the feel of her if she kept annoying him. 'You were saying something about men like me?'

He knelt at her feet and unzipped one of her boots.

'Yes,' she said, and her voice was only a touch uneven. 'Men who only want one thing from a woman and then discard them when they're finished.'

'That "one thing" being sex, I take it?' He put the boot aside and set to work on the other one.

'Yes, I'm sure you do,' she bit out scornfully. 'Take it, that is.'

He looked up to find her studying the ceiling. 'This is hardly *taking it*, Lily,' he retorted gruffly. 'And let's just say I'm not enjoying this either—but I don't usually entertain possible drug felons, so you'll have to excuse my current *modus operandi*.'

'I'll excuse nothing,' she spat.

'And—' he stopped, completely losing his train of thought when he found his face on a level with that part of her body he'd love to touch. To taste.

Was she as aroused as he was? Wet even?

Hell, don't go there. Just don't go there.

He blanked his mind as much as possible as he ran both hands up over one long, lean leg, finally remembering what he was about to say. 'And I've never had a woman complain.'

'That's not true.'

He stopped and looked at her.

'I remember reading about that girl. A model who said that you tricked her into thinking you cared. That you wouldn't know love if it…if it hit—no, knocked you on the head.'

Tristan paused. 'She's entitled to her opinion, but it wasn't my fault she fell in love with me. She knew exactly what type of relationship she was getting into, and love was never part of the deal.'

'Silly girl.' Lily folded her arms across her chest and stared anywhere but at him. 'She doesn't know how lucky she was. Personally, I don't know any woman in her right mind who could ever imagine being in love with you.'

He shifted to her other leg.

'Unfortunately it happens. But women fall in love with many things, and it's rarely the man they see in front of them.' And in him, he knew, they saw a title and a life of privilege. Like his mother had with his father. *Shopping, champagne and chauffeurs,* he'd heard her brag to more than one friend.

'You should be thankful they want something at all. It's not like you can rely on your charming personality,' she scorned.

Tristan laughed—a hard sound in the deathly silent room. 'I'm not looking for love.' He rose and reached around to cup her bottom, closing his eyes as he slid both hands into her deep back pockets.

Lily's hands flew to his chest, as if to hold him back, but how easy would it be just to tug her forward and let her feel how much she aroused him?

'What happened?' She gasped breathlessly. 'Did a woman scorn you, Tristan?'

He knew she was deliberately trying to distract him, and that she was right to do so.

'No woman's ever got close enough to scorn me, Honey,' he sneered, skating his hands along the inside of her waistband and then finally cupping between her legs.

'You bastard!' she seethed, her hand rising to slap his face.

He stopped her, but deep down he knew he deserved it. He let her go so she could stalk to the opposite side of the bed.

'I hope you're satisfied.'

Not by a long shot, sweetheart.

'That was necessary. Nothing else,' he said evenly.

'Keep telling yourself that. It might make you sleep better tonight,' she spat.

'I'll sleep just fine,' he lied.

'Well, you shouldn't. But I'm curious—is it just me you don't trust, or all women?'

'Don't go there.'

'Why not? Your attitude is abysmal for someone whose parents were happily married—'

'Actually, my parents weren't happily married.'

'They weren't?' She blinked in surprise.

'No. I don't think my mother ever really loved my father and he refused to see it. Which was to his detriment in the end, because as soon as she got a better offer she took off.'

'Oh, that's terrible.' Her automatic compassion was like a fist to his stomach.

'Yeah, well, that wasn't the worst of it. Love has a way of making fools of us all. Something to remember.'

He turned sharply on his heel and strode from her room before he did something stupid. Like throw her on the bed and give her what he knew they both wanted—no matter how much she tried to deny it.

Once in his room, Tristan shed his clothes and jumped into the shower, turning the mixer all the way to cold and dousing his head as if it was on fire. He let the freezing water wash over him for a minute and then reset the temperature to hot. God, that search… He blew out a breath. The more he tried to control his physical reaction to her the more out of control it seemed to become.

This situation was seriously driving him crazy.

She was seriously driving him crazy. And, worse, the memory of the day his mother had walked out on them wouldn't leave him alone.

Tristan had overheard his parents arguing. Overheard his mother telling his father that he had nothing she wanted. That her son, Tristan, had nothing she wanted either. And that had bitten deep, because every time she had spiralled downwards Tristan had always been there to try and help her. Tried to be there for her. So to have her only want Jordana...

The memory still chilled his blood. It had taken him a long time to realise that no one was good enough for her and that all those years of trying to win her love and approval had been for nothing.

He scrubbed his hand over his face and shut the mixer off. He pulled on silk boxer shorts and walked up the outdoor circular staircase to his rooftop balcony.

The night was cool, and he enjoyed the sting of air on his skin as he leaned on the wrought-iron railing and looked out over the dark mass that was the Heath and the twinkling coloured lights of London beyond. The cumulus clouds that hung over the city had a faint pinkish tinge due to the light pollution, but he barely noticed. His mind was focused on replaying the day's events in his head.

Which wasn't a good thing—because his head was full of more questions than answers.

He didn't know whether to believe Lily about her not having a current lover, but he was beginning to suspect that she was telling the truth about not knowing she'd had drugs in her bag. That was disconcerting, because it meant he'd been wrong about her. He couldn't remember the last time he'd been wrong about a person. Hated to think that he was now. Because if he was he owed her an apology.

Could she really be as genuine, as *untouched,* as she appeared? Or was he just a fool, being taken in by a beautiful and duplicitous woman? One whose job it was to pretend to be someone she wasn't.

Whatever she was, he desired her more than he'd desired any woman before—and that wasn't good.

He gripped the balustrade so tightly his palms hurt. He needed an outlet for all the pent-up energy whizzing through his blood, and the only thing he could think of to assuage his physical ache was totally off-limits.

Straightening, he clasped his hands behind his neck, twisting his body from side to side to ease the kinks in his back. A run usually helped clear the cobwebs away. And if he didn't have a suspect movie star sleeping next door he'd put on his joggers and do exactly that. But then, if he *didn't* have a suspect movie star sleeping next door he probably wouldn't need to go for a run at—he glanced at his watch—one in the morning.

Grimacing, he strode inside and flopped face down on his bed.

Given that he couldn't get rid of her in the short term, the only way he could think of to deal with this situation was with the detached professionalism he would offer any client and ignore the attraction between them.

He'd told her more than once today that he was in charge, and damn it if he wasn't going to start behaving as if he was tomorrow.

CHAPTER EIGHT

'A MOVIE premiere? Is this your idea of a joke?'

Tristan's PA flinched as she stood on the other side of his desk, and he realised he'd said almost those exact words to his sister at almost this exact time yesterday.

Again he'd been having a great morning, and again it was shot to—

Okay, so it hadn't been *that* great a morning, what with Lily waking up late and a police detective waiting around in his home until she did so, but it was definitely ruined now. He cut a hard look to Lily, who stared back impassively at him from the white sofa.

'Uh, n-no,' Kate stuttered.

He glanced back at his computer screen, at the images Kate had brought up of the legions of fans who had camped out overnight in Leicester Square to get a glimpse of Lily Wild at some premiere to be held that evening.

'Lily, tell me this is a joke.'

He watched Lily's throat work as she swallowed, and then he returned his eyes to his surprised PA, who didn't seem to know what to do with her hands.

She'd never seen him on the verge of losing his temper before and she was clearly daunted.

'I wasn't going to say anything,' Lily informed him coolly, standing to walk over to his desk.

Only she wasn't so cool deep down, because she didn't seem to know what to do with her hands either, and nervously pleated the loose folds of her peasant skirt.

His eyes swept upwards over her clinging purple shirt and then into eyes almost the same shade. 'I'm sure you weren't,' he mocked.

'Only because I was going to cancel my attendance—not because I didn't want you to know about it.'

Cancel it? He doubted that very much. She'd set up her attendance long before now, and while she might be feeling apprehensive about her drug bust he doubted she seriously wanted to miss an opportunity in the limelight. She'd chosen that life, after all.

'Oh, you can't cancel!' Kate cried, trying very hard not to appear starstruck. 'The premiere was delayed until today so you could make it, and there are people who have camped out in the cold night to see you. They'll be so disappointed. Look.'

She pointed to the computer screen, but Tristan's eyes stayed locked on Lily's face.

Just as they did later that night, when he found himself in the back of his limousine being whisked through central London on his way to Leicester Square.

It wasn't quite sunset, but the sky was filled with leaden clouds that blocked the setting sun from view and made it darker than it otherwise would be. Light rain splattered the windows, and Tristan wondered if Lily looked so nervous because she was worried that the rain would ruin the look she and Jordana had come up with in his bathroom or something else.

Because she certainly looked nervous.

Her chest was rising and falling with each deep, almost meditative breath she took. Her hands were locked together in her lap, and with her eyes closed she looked like Marie Antoinette must have before being dragged to the guillotine. But he didn't think Marie Antoinette could have looked anywhere near as beautiful as Lily Wild did at this minute. As she did every damned minute.

Then the car rounded the final bend and he suspected he knew why she might be nervous.

The car pulled up kerbside, and the door was immediately opened by a burly security guard wearing a glow-in-the-dark red-and-yellow bomber jacket. A wide red carpet extended in front of them for miles, dividing the screaming mass of fans barely constrained behind waist-high barricades.

Men and women in suits trawled the carpet, and the fans went from wild to berserk, waving books and posters around like flags, as Lily alighted from the car into a pool of spotlights.

The stage lighting on nearby buildings and trees was no match for the sea of camera flashes that blinded Lily, and then himself, on both sides as Tristan followed Lily out of the car.

An official photographer rushed up and started snapping Lily from every angle, while a woman in a dark suit and clipboard motioned her along the carpet to sign autographs for the waiting fans.

Tristan felt as if he'd stepped into an alternative universe, and wasn't wholly comfortable when Lily approached one of the barricades and the fans surged forward as one, making the beefy security guards who could have moonlighted as linebackers for the New Zealand All Blacks square off menacingly.

Tristan felt sure the fans were about to break through the barricades, and his own muscles bunched in readiness to grab Lily and haul her behind him if that should happen.

In the surrounding sea of multiple colours and broad black umbrellas held aloft to ward off the fine rain falling from the sky Lily stood out with her cream-coloured dress, lightly golden skin and up-swept silvery-blond hair.

When he had first seen her in the dress Jordana had produced earlier—a knee-length clinging sheath with a high neck—he'd known he was in trouble. Then she had turned to reveal that it had no back, and he'd nearly told her to go back and put on her blouse and peasant skirt. But then he'd have had to explain why, and he didn't like admitting why to himself let alone anyone else.

Now he could appreciate that Jordana had wrought

a small miracle, and had made Lily look like a golden angel amid a sea of darkness.

Which, aesthetically, was wonderful, but was not so great for his personal comfort level—nor, he could safely say, that of any other man who happened to look upon her that night!

He watched her now, doing her thing with the fans, and thought back over the interminable day.

All day she had been a paragon of virtue. She'd done exactly as he wanted—sat on the white sofa in his office and acted as if she wasn't there. Which should have made it easier to ignore her but hadn't. Because while she had immersed herself in a script with all the verve of someone preparing to sit a final exam he had struggled to find one case that held his attention long enough for him to forget she was in the room.

When he'd tried to engage her in a conversation about what had happened the night of Jo's eighteenth birthday party she had clammed up, and he had to wonder why. Jordana had implied that he'd been wrong about Lily's involvement, but if so why would Lily remain tight-lipped and only throw him that phony smile of hers when he broached the topic?

A roar from the crowd snapped his head around as a tall, buff Latino heart-throb dressed in torn jeans and a crumpled shirt swaggered towards Lily, raising both hands to wave at the near-hysterical crowd as he went. Lily turned and swatted the man with her million-dollar smile and Tristan felt his insides clench. That smile was like the midday sun coming out from behind heavy clouds—bright and instantly warming. Seductive and impossible to ignore. And so genuine it made his jaw harden. She had yet to turn it his way again, and he realised that he wanted her to. Badly.

The heart-throb draped his arm around Lily's waist and leaned in to kiss her, smiling at her like some long-lost lover.

They looked good together, his dark hair a perfect foil for her blondeness, and Tristan's eyes narrowed as he watched them work the crowd. His initial instinct to leap forward and rip the actor's arm from its socket slowly abated as he calmed his senses and realised that the actor's light touches here and there were too tentative to be that of a lover.

If the guy had known her intimately he wouldn't be just placing his hand on her hip now and then for a photo. He'd be subtly spreading his fingers wide over the small of her back, which Tristan already knew was sensitive to a man's touch. He'd let his fingers trail the naked baby-soft skin there and smile into her eyes when she delicately shuddered in response. Maybe he'd even press lightly on her flesh to have her arch ever so slightly towards him. Maybe exert just enough pressure so that he could hear that soft hitch in her breath as her mouth parted—

Hell.

Tristan pulled his thoughts back from the brink and dug his hands into his pockets, calling himself an idiot and wondering how long he could continue like this.

The crowd gave a howl of complaint as Lily and the heart-throb walked back towards the red carpet. The actor's hand hovered behind her protectively, and even though Tristan knew they weren't lovers he could tell by the expression on the Latino's face that he'd probably give up that arm to become so.

He was immensely irritated by the man's proprietorial air—and by his own desire to possess her. Especially when she had done little to incite his attention. And why hadn't she?

Lily Wild was turning out to be an enigma, and he was not at all happy to find that he might have been guilty of stereotyping her just as much as the next person.

'I have to do the red carpet thing and answer a few questions from the press and then we can go in,' she murmured over the noise of the crowd.

He nodded, but his eyes were on the actor, and Tristan found himself deliberately stepping into Lily's personal space to let the heart-throb know she was off-limits.

Lily's eyes widened quizzically, but the actor got the message, throwing his chest forward in a display of machismo.

They took each other's measure for a beat, and then the actor gave a typically Mediterranean shrug.

'Hey, man, don't sweat it.' He laughed, backing down when it became obvious that Tristan wouldn't.

'I was just helping Angel, here. You know how she gets in crowds.'

Tristan didn't, but he nodded anyway and watched the heart-throb amble further along the line.

He put his hand on Lily's arm to stop her following. 'What was he talking about?'

Lily sniffed, and raised a hand to wave at her fans. 'Nothing.'

He tightened his grip as she made to shrug him off. 'How was he helping you?'

'Not by feeding me drugs, if that's what you're thinking.'

He hadn't been thinking that, and her comment ticked him off. 'Then tell me what he was talking about.'

'I can't explain here.' She nodded to a fellow actor who blew a hello kiss. 'I don't have time.'

'Make time.'

'Oh!' She huffed, and then leaned closer to him, her delicate perfume wafting into his sinuses. 'I used to have agoraphobia. Now can we go?'

Tristan frowned. 'Fear of open spaces?'

'Do you even know *how* to whisper?' she complained, clearly uncomfortable with the subject matter. 'Most people think of it as that, but in my case it's a fear of crowds and being trapped in a situation I can't control.'

'That's what the therapy was about?' he said.

She glanced at him sharply. 'How do you know…?

Oh, your special investigator's report. Well, it's nice to know he got some things right.'

'How do you know it was a he?'

'Because from the little I know of what's in it he's made snap judgements on very little evidence at all—just like a man.'

Tristan bit back a response and refocused. 'How bad is your phobia?'

Lily sighed. 'It's not bad at all. Jordi Mantuso and I swapped stories on set and he was just being kind.'

Tristan was shocked by her revelation. 'And are you okay? Right now?'

She looked taken aback by the question and he gritted his teeth, realising that his behaviour towards her had given her a very negative impression of who he was.

'Y-yes. I'm okay. It's not like I can't go out in a crowd—it's more a fear of being trapped by them.'

'Like when you were a child and surrounded with your parents' crowds of fans?'

The softness that had come over her face at his concern disappeared, and she looked away before glancing back. 'Yes. They think that's where it started. But I haven't had an attack in years.'

One of the female minders approached, to find out what was delaying them, and Tristan watched Lily paste on a smile that didn't reach her eyes as she walked towards the rows of paparazzi.

She answered questions and posed for photographs like the professional she was, and he couldn't help respecting the adversity she had learned to overcome in order to work in her chosen profession.

He could see her making moves to finish up, and then her body stiffened. Something was wrong. Was she having a panic attack?

'I don't do theatre,' she was saying firmly.

'But why not, Lily? You've been offered the role of a lifetime, playing your mum. Are you not even considering it?'

'No.' Polite, but definite.

'What's wrong with the U.K., Lily? Don't you like us?'

'Of course.' Another pretty smile that didn't quite reach her eyes. 'My schedule hasn't allowed me to return to England before now.'

'The roles you choose…' an oily voice spoke up from the rear and paused for effect '…they're very different women from your mother. Is that a deliberate decision on your part? Is that why you won't take the West End gig?'

Lily felt Tristan step closer, and the warmth from his body momentarily distracted her from the reporter's question. She hated this part of the proceedings. And she wouldn't take the part playing her mother if it was the last known acting role on the planet.

'I choose my roles according to what interests me. My current film, *Carried Away,* is a romantic comedy, and…I like happy endings…what else can I say?' Lily smiled and turned to answer another question about location, before the same reporter who had been taking potshots at her from the get-go piped up again.

'Do you ever worry about being thought of as like your mother?'

'No.' Lily's smile felt as if it was made of cardboard and she thought about making an exit.

'What's it like kissing Jordi Mantuso?'

'Divine.' Lily's smile was genuine, and the fans who had caught her words whooped.

But the oily guy was back. 'Miss Wild, I'm still not clear about the West End gig. We've heard the director is holding off signing another female lead, so is the reason you won't do it because you're worried about the theatre aspect or...something else?'

Oh, this guy was good. He was a top-of-the-line paparazzo with a nose for a juicy story, and Lily could feel some of that old panic from years ago—the panic she had just told Tristan was firmly under control—well up inside her.

It was being back in London that was doing it. The whole stigma of who her parents had been. And the paps here were relentless. She rarely had to face such insolence in other parts of the world.

The reporter's question had become jumbled in her head and she was struggling to swallow when she felt Tristan's hand snake around her lower back and rest possessively over her hipbone; his fingers spread wide, almost stroking her through her the delicate fabric of her dress.

She felt a flush heat her face as her stomach muscles trembled, and fervently hoped he wouldn't notice either response.

She tried to turn and silently berate him, but his fingers held her in place. His breath stirred the wisps of hair coiling around her temple as he leaned in closer and stole the breath from her lungs.

'You've forgotten he's a slimeball and you're taking his question seriously. Just look up at me as if I've said something incredibly funny and ignore him.'

He let her half turn in the circle of his arms, but she couldn't force the response he'd suggested.

Her hand automatically came up between them and flattened against the black designer shirt Jordana had provided him with. Her fingers curled into the fabric. She didn't know if she was trying to hold him back or draw him closer, because her brain had frozen at the open hunger banked in his direct gaze.

The noise of the crowd, the cameras, the lights… everything faded as Lily felt suffused with warmth and a sexual need that was as debilitating as it was exciting.

She felt his swift indrawn breath as she held his gaze, and was powerless to look away when his eyes dropped to her mouth.

Dimly she became aware of the crowd chanting, 'Kiss! Kiss!' and as if in slow motion a soft smile curved Tristan's firm mouth.

He leaned in and gently touched his lips to hers. The soft contact was fleeting, but still her lips clung, and as he pulled back and looked at her she knew he'd felt her unbidden response. He stared at her as if he wanted more—and if he didn't the screaming fans certainly did.

Lily's fingernails flexed, and somehow she found the wherewithal to pull back, once again becoming aware of the whistles and wild catcalls of 'Who is he?' and 'Is that Lord Garrett?' from the press.

The camera flashes were relentless, and Lily knew that while Tristan's actions had been motivated purely to help her out of an awkward moment, hers had not.

And wishing it was otherwise wouldn't make it so.

CHAPTER NINE

'I ENJOYED the film,' Tristan said, breaking the heavy silence between them. Lily didn't look at him but continued to stare out of the window as his chauffeur drove them through the glistening London streets.

It was late, and after two hours of sitting beside Tristan in a darkened movie theatre she felt uptight and edgy. The awareness she had been trying to keep at bay by pretending to read that hateful play for most of the day had exploded the minute his lips had touched hers on the red carpet.

No doubt he'd felt sorry for her after her earlier disclosure, but that didn't stop her from wanting him to touch her because he wanted to, not out of some misplaced duty to look out for her.

And she didn't want to make polite small talk with him now. She just wanted to get to the safety of her room and go to bed. To sleep.

In hindsight she should have been more prepared for the intrusive questions of the U.K. press, and probably would have been if worry over her case and the tension between herself and Tristan wasn't taking up so much head space.

Of course that brief kiss would be headline news in the papers tomorrow. Would be on the internet right now in this era of instantaneous news reports!

She knew she shouldn't be angry about what he'd done. He'd only been trying to help. But her own response to his sensitivity both now and this morning, when he'd made a Scotland Yard detective wait two hours until she woke from an exhausted sleep, and yesterday when he'd eased her headache while she slept in the car, made it harder for her to keep ignoring her feelings for him.

Especially after his disclosure about his parents and the pain in his voice when he had referred to his mother. The knowledge that he'd been hurt as a child made Lily feel differently towards him. Made her want to soothe him. To find out what had been worse than his mother leaving. Feeling this way about him wasn't clever. It could only lead to heartache—her own!

She sighed heavily and felt his gaze linger on her. She really didn't want to have any reason to lessen the animosity between them. Without that it would be far too easy to fall back into her adolescent fantasy that he was her dream man. What she needed to remember was that deep down he was essentially a good person, but any solicitude he extended towards her didn't automatically cancel out what he really thought of her.

'No comment, Lily?'

And he was calling her Lily now, instead of Honey. Oh, she *really* didn't want him being nice to her.

'You shouldn't have done that before,' she berated him, letting her embarrassment and uncertainty at this whole situation between them take centre stage.

He glanced at her briefly. 'Tell you I enjoyed your film?'

'Divert attention away from that reporter on the red carpet by kissing me.'

His direct gaze made her nervous, so she focused on the darkened buildings as the big car sped along Finchley Road.

'You looked like you needed it,' he said softly.

'I didn't.' Lily knew she was being argumentative, but she couldn't seem to stop herself. 'And now your picture—*our* picture—is going to be splashed all over the papers tomorrow. They'll think we're lovers.'

The car pulled up outside his exclusive mansion and he turned to her before opening the door. 'They'd probably have assumed that anyway given that I accompanied you.'

Bert opened the door and Lily smiled her thanks to him before stalking after Tristan, annoyance at his cavalier attitude radiating through her. 'Assuming and confirming isn't the same thing,' she retorted. Realizing too late what her words implied, she hoped he wouldn't pick up on it.

Movement further up the street alerted them to a lurking photographer, and Lily allowed Tristan to usher her up the short walkway to the black double front doors that looked as if they shone with boot polish.

He pushed one open and she preceded him into the marble foyer, and then followed him through to the large dining room where he turned to face her.

'Interesting phrasing. But I'm not sure how I could have confirmed something that's not true?' he drawled, a dangerous gleam lighting his eyes.

'Oh, you know what I mean,' she said, flustered by the strength of her confusing emotions. 'I'm tired.'

'Is that your way of defending your Freudian slip?'

'It wasn't…' She noted his raised eyebrow and swore. 'Oh, go to hell,' Lily fired at him, walking ahead of him through to the vast sitting room, dominated by a king-sized sofa that faced plate-glass windows overlooking the city.

'You know, all this outraged indignation over my attempt to help you before seems a little excessive to me,' Tristan said from behind her.

Lily turned, her eyes drawn to his lean, muscular elegance as he propped up the doorway even though she was determined not to be drawn in by his brooding masculinity. 'Oh, really?'

Tristan leant against the doorjamb and studied Lily's defiant posture. Her face was flushed, and more wisps of hair had escaped her bun and were kissing her neck. Her lips were pouting, and he'd bet his life savings that she'd crossed her arms over her chest to hide her arousal from him. He knew why she was so angry. He knew she felt the sexual pull between them and was as enthralled by it as he was.

And, while she might be upset with the media fall-out from his actions on the red carpet, he hadn't missed the way her lips had clung to his and how her violet eyes had blazed with instantaneous desire when he'd kissed her.

'Yes, really. Want me to tell you what I think is behind it?' he asked benignly.

'Pure, unadulterated hatred.' She faked a yawn and he laughed.

'You know what they say about hatred, Lily.' Tristan stalked over to the drinks cabinet and threw a measure of whisky into a glass. Two days with her and he was beginning to feel like an alcoholic!

'Yes, it means you don't like someone. And my reaction to your behaviour is not excessive in the slightest. All you've done tonight is give the tabloids more fodder—and for your information I could have handled that reporter by myself.'

Tristan raised his glass and swallowed the fiery liquid in one go, welcoming the sharp bite of distraction from the turn the conversation had taken. All he'd done was compliment her performance!

'Was that before or after you had the panic attack?' he asked silkily.

'It wasn't a panic attack! And just because I tell you something personal it doesn't mean you get to take over. You're not God's gift—even though you clearly think you are.'

Tristan turned slowly and stared at her. He'd heard the clear note of challenge in her voice and he knew the reason for it. And, by God, if he didn't want to do something about it—regardless of everything that lay between them.

He wanted her, and he knew for damned sure she wanted him, and looking at her right now, with her legs slightly apart and her hands fisted on her hips, her chin thrust out, he knew she wanted him to do something about it too.

Not that she would admit it.

He let his eyes slide slowly down her body and then just as slowly all the way back up. The pulse-point in her throat leapt to life, but she made no attempt to run from the hunger he knew was burning holes in his retinas.

There was something interminably innocent about her provocative stance, almost as if she didn't know what she was about, and it pulled him up for a minute. But then he discounted the notion. She might not be the Jezebel he thought she was, but women like Lily Wild always knew what they were about. He'd had enough of the simmering tension between them, and knew just how to kill it dead.

'Okay, that's it,' he said softly, placing his empty glass on the antique sideboard with deliberate care. 'I'm giving you fair warning. I'm sick of the tension between us—and the reason for it. You've got exactly three seconds to get moving before I take up from what we started six years ago. But this time there'll be no stopping. You're not seventeen any more, and there's no secretary to interrupt us like yesterday. This time we're on our own, and I'm not in the mind to stop at one kiss. Neither, I suspect, are you.'

Lily didn't know what thrilled her more—his blunt words or the starkly masculine arousal stamped across his handsome face. Her heart took off at full gallop and her stomach pitched alarmingly.

Six years ago she had wanted him with the desperate yearning of a teenager in the throes of a first crush. The night of Jo's party she had dressed for him, watched him, noticed him watching her—and then, on the back of a couple of fortifying glasses of vintage champagne, she had asked him to dance... and melted into him. Loved the feel of his strong arms around her, the sense of rightness that would have led her to do anything with him that night. And right now she felt exactly the same way. Which just didn't make sense. None of this made sense.

Does it have to?

'One.'

She shook her head. 'Tristan, don't be ridiculous. There's no point to this.'

'I couldn't agree more, but we have unfinished business between us and denying it hasn't made it go away. Nor has trying to ignore it. In fact, I think that's only made the problem worse.'

'And you think acting on it will solve it?'

He raised that arrogant eyebrow. 'Got a better idea?'

No, she didn't, and right now her body yearned for his with a desperation that was all-consuming. Yearned to experience more of the pleasure he'd wrought on her body yesterday. Yearned for a completion that Lily was starting to suspect only this man could fulfil.

Jordana's provocative suggestion that she cut loose and have some fun returned to mock her.

Could she?

Would having sex with Tristan fall under that banner? It wasn't as if she was holding out for a marriage proposal or anything. The only reason she hadn't had sex before was because of the lack of opportunity and…enticement. She'd never felt the way Tristan made her feel just by looking at him. Why keep denying it?

And then there was the notion she'd had to meet him this trip as an equal. To put the attraction she had always felt for him to bed…

'Two.'

His soft voice cut through her ruminations and she realised her heart was pounding behind her ribcage.

She swallowed. He hadn't moved, and yet the room seemed smaller; he seemed closer. Her senses were entirely focused on him.

His hair had flopped forward and she could see he was breathing as unevenly as she was. She found it almost shockingly exciting to think she could arouse a man like him to such a state. Because he *was* aroused. She could see the unchecked desire glittering in his darkened eyes and feel the dangerous intensity of his tautly held body.

Her stomach clenched and she felt an answering hunger in herself at the thought of finally being able to touch all that roughly hewn muscle. So what was she waiting for? Armageddon?

Lily slicked her tongue over her arid lips, a nascent sense of her own feminine power heating her insides and making her breasts feel firmer, fuller.

He must have sensed her silent capitulation because he moved then, pacing towards her with the latent grace of a man who knew exactly what he was about, and any notions Lily had had of taking charge of their lovemaking flew out of the window. She felt like that inexperienced seventeen-year-old again in comparison to him and his wealth of sexual experience.

He stopped just short of touching her and Lily gazed into his face with nervous anticipation.

'Tristan…' Her voice was a whisper of uncertainty and for a second her inner voice told her she was mad. She couldn't possibly give this giant of a man what he needed.

Tristan reached out and curled his hand around the nape of her neck, angling her face to his. He stared at her for what felt like ages. 'Tell me you want this.'

His warm fingers sent shock waves of energy up

and down her spine and Lily was breathing so hard she was almost hyperventilating.

Want it? Need it sounded closer to the mark.

'I do.' She ran her tongue over her dry lips. 'I do want this. You.'

She heard an almost pained sound come from Tristan's throat as he lifted her face to his and took her mouth in a searing kiss. No preliminaries required.

Both his hands spread wide either side of her face as he held her still beneath his plundering lips and tongue.

Lily felt a sob of pure need rise up in her throat and reached up to grip his broad shoulders, to hang on as she gave herself over to the sensation of his masterful kiss.

He tasted of whisky and heaven, and for a moment Lily's senses nearly shut down with the overload of sensation rioting through her.

She pulled back, gasping for breath as she realised the dizziness was from a lack of oxygen, hyperventilating for real now as he angled her head back and skated his lips across her jaw and down the smooth column of her neck.

'Oh, Lord…' Lily whimpered, her face nuzzling his to bring his mouth back to her own.

He gave a husky chuckle and acquiesced, kissing her with such unrestrained passion she thought she might faint. His big body moved in, pressing her into the wall behind her.

His kiss claimed her. Branded her. The hard wall was flat against her back as his equally hard chest moulded to her front.

She moved her hands into his hair and lifted herself to try and assuage the ache that had grown to almost painful proportions between her thighs.

One of his hands disentangled from her hair and found the naked skin at small of her back as he stumbled back slightly at her eager movements.

'Oh, Lily, you're killing me,' he groaned into her mouth, his hands not quite steady as he held her in place against him.

His touch seemed as if it was everywhere and nowhere, and Lily could feel all her old emotions for this man welling up inside her. She couldn't have stopped what was happening now even if she'd wanted to.

She shivered and arched into his caresses, moving restlessly against him as wanton pleasure consumed her. His touch was electric, but it wasn't enough. She wanted to feel him all around her, and inside that part of her that somehow felt soft and hollow and unbearably empty.

'Tristan, please...' Lily implored, her hands kneading the hard ridges of his upper back. He seemed to know what she needed because he brought his mouth back to hers, his tongue plunging inside as his leg pressed firmly between her thighs.

She felt a moment's relief—but her dress hampered him from putting more pressure where she wanted it most and she squirmed in frustration.

Keeping her upright with his thigh, Tristan brought both hands up to cup her breasts, and then higher to drag the shoulders of her dress down her arms, baring her to the waist. Lily held her breath as he pulled back an inch and looked at her with such heated desire she could have wept.

For the first time ever she truly felt like a goddess, and when his eyes met hers they were dark with barely checked need.

'Honey, I want to go slow, but…' His eyes dropped back to her breasts and he placed his hands either side of her ribcage, lifted her body to meet his mouth. 'You're exquisite,' he whispered, his hot breath skating across an aroused nipple just before his mouth opened and sucked her flesh into its moist cavern.

Her legs gave out and Tristan had to tighten the arm around her waist to hold her up. Damp heat flooded between her thighs and she could dimly hear someone panting Tristan's name in a litany. She realised it was her.

She stopped, tried to centre herself, and then he grazed her with his teeth and she felt her insides convulse.

'Don't stop,' he breathed urgently against her flesh. 'Say my name. Tell me what you like.'

Lily didn't know what she liked, except for everything he was doing to her, and she gave herself over to him as he shifted his attention to her other breast, digging her nails into her palms. Wanting, needing to touch him as he was touching her.

She tried to move her arms and gave a mew of frustration when she found they were trapped by the tight band of his arms and her dress.

'Help me...' she began, but he already was, pressing his thigh firmly against her and moving his arms so she could disentangle her hands.

Once free, she immediately set to work on the buttons of his dark shirt.

He was breathing just as hard as she was, and a fine sheen had broken out over the skin her jittery hands were having trouble exposing. Then he raised both hands to her breasts to tug at her nipples and Lily's fingers fumbled to a stop.

'That's not helping,' she groaned, involuntarily arching into his caress.

'Then allow me.' Tristan grabbed hold of his shirt and tore the rest of the buttons free, leaning in close before she was able to look her fill of his sculptured chest, his ridged abdomen. Then his chest hair scraped her sensitised nipples, and she forgot about looking as feeling took precedence.

'Oh, God...' Lily swayed and rocked against the rigid length of him pressed into her belly.

'Easy, Honey,' Tristan soothed, but Lily was beyond easy. She needed him to touch her between her legs. The ache there was now unbearable.

She groaned with relief when she felt his hands smooth over her thighs and ruch her dress up around her waist, her legs automatically widening to accommodate his seeking hand.

His movements seemed as unsteady as she felt, and it imbued her with a sense of power.

Unable to keep her mouth off him, she bent her head and licked along his neck, breathing in his earthy masculinity.

'Tristan, please, I need you,' Lily begged, her voice sounding hoarse. Another saner voice was telling her that later she'd be embarrassed by such uninhibited pleading. But her body couldn't care less about later on.

It was caught up in the most delicious lassitude and straining for something that seemed just out of reach.

Then his fingers whispered over the very tops of her upper thigh and the feeling came closer. A lot closer.

Lily's breath stalled and her body stilled, and when finally he slipped his fingers beneath the lacy edge of her barely there panties and stroked through the curls that guarded her femininity she nearly died, clinging to his broad shoulders. Her body was his to do with as he willed.

And he did. His fingers slipped easily over her flesh, unerringly finding the tight bud of her clitoris before pressing deeper. Stretching her with first one and then two fingers.

A groan that seemed to come from the very centre of his body tore from his mouth. 'Honey, you're so wet. So tight.' He seemed lost for a second, and then established a rhythm within her that created a rush of heat to the centre of her body. But suddenly he stopped.

'No, I want to be inside you when you come.' He pulled his hand free and Lily's nails dug into his shoulders in protest.

She heard the metallic sound of his belt buckle and the slide of his zipper and in seconds he was back.

Only her panties were in the way, and with a decisive movement they went the way of his shirt.

Lily followed an age-old instinct and rocked against him, her mouth on his neck, her hands in the thick lusciousness of his hair.

'Honey, you keep that up and this will be over before I'm even inside you,' he said hoarsely, stroking his tongue into her open mouth. He eased back, seeming to remember where they were. 'Not here though.'

'Yes, here.' Lily demanded against his mouth, an urgent excitement driving her beyond the edge of reason.

Her lower body felt as if it was contracting around thin air and she needed him inside her. Filling her.

Tristan sucked in an uneven breath and lowered both hands to cup her bottom, lifting her into him. 'Put your legs around my waist,' he instructed gruffly, and Lily blindly obeyed as the velveteen tip of his body nudged against the very centre of hers.

The back of his neck was taut and sweaty and Lily's head fell forward and she nipped at his salty skin. He must have liked it, because with a sound that was part pain, part pleasure, he tilted her body towards him and surged into her in one single, powerful thrust.

For a second the world stopped, and then Lily registered a harsh cry and realised she must have bitten down on Tristan's neck—hard—as her body initially resisted his vigorous invasion.

He swore viciously and instantly stilled, reefing his head back and cupping her face in one hand to pull her eyes to his.

'Honey, please tell me this isn't your first time.'

Lily felt the momentary sting pass as her body stretched to accommodate his fullness, and wrapped her arms tightly around his neck.

'Don't stop,' she breathed as her body completely surrendered to his and tiny sparks of pleasure returned between her thighs.

She shifted to try and elevate the feeling, but Tristan's fingers dug into her hips to keep her still. 'Wait. Let your body adjust to me.'

'It has,' she insisted, and felt his slightly damp hair brush her face as he shook his head.

'Please, Tristan, I need to—'

He rocked against her and Lily moaned the word *move* as if it had six syllables.

Tristan eased in and out of her body gently, and then with more urgency, and Lily's brain shut down. All she could do was feel as a thrilling tightness swept through her and urged her on. Then Tristan moved one hand up between their bodies and lightly stroked his thumb over her nipple, and Lily's world splintered apart as pleasure clamped her body to his.

Tristan swore again, and thrust into her with such force all Lily could do was wrap her arms around his neck and hang on as he claimed her body with his and reached his own nirvana.

After what felt like an hour Lily became conscious of how her uneven breathing was pressing her newly sensitised breasts into the soft hair on Tristan's chest, and also of how hard the wall was behind her—despite the fact that Tristan had curled his arm around her back to take the brunt of the pressure.

She was also conscious that Tristan still had his mouth buried against her neck, his lips pressed lightly against her skin as he tried to regulate his own breathing.

Her arms were slung laxly over his shoulders and a feeling of utter contentment enveloped her. A sense of euphoria was curling through her insides like warm chocolate syrup.

It was madness. This inexplicable feeling of completeness that swelled in her chest. But maybe it was because she'd had a life-changing experience. And she had. Nothing had prepared her for what had just happened. No song. No movie. No book. And she knew she'd remember this moment for ever.

But even through her high she could discern that Tristan wasn't feeling the same way. He was unnaturally still, his breathing too laboured, as if he was having trouble composing himself. She shifted then, and the hardness of the wall scraped her skin. The air was slightly chilly now, as the sweat started to dry on her body. She shivered, still supported by his strong arms. Muscles she'd never felt before contracted around his hardness, still buried deep inside her, and she flinched as he cursed.

He pulled out of her, gently lowering her to the parquetry floor, stepping back. A look of abject disgust lined his face.

The shock of it made Lily recoil, and she quickly dropped her eyes and dragged her crumpled dress into place.

She heard him readjust his own clothing, and a primeval survival instinct she had honed as a child took root inside as she blanked out the feeling of utter desolation that threatened to overwhelm her for the first time in years.

'Don't say anything,' she ordered, knowing that the best form of defence was attack, and was mildly surprised when shock replaced the revulsion she had seen on his face.

Good. She might not be as practised as he was in these post-sex matters, but pride demanded that she did not behave like the bumbling fool she now felt.

For him this was just run of the mill but for her it was—

'*Don't say anything?*' he all but bellowed. 'You should have told me you were a virgin.'

Never let 'em know you care, Honeybee.

She looked at him levelly. 'It slipped my mind.' In truth she had hoped he wouldn't notice. But that seemed like a stupid notion in hindsight, given his size. 'And you wouldn't have believed me anyway, would you?'

He glanced to the side and it was all the answer Lily needed. Of course he wouldn't have—when had he ever believed her? Something tight clutched in her chest and she toed on the shoe that had fallen off when her legs had been wrapped around his lean hips.

'I didn't use a condom,' he said, the bald statement bringing her eyes back to his.

She wasn't on the pill. Why would she be?

'I think it's a safe time,' she murmured automatically, trying to quell a sense of panic so she could think about when her last period had been.

He groaned and paced away from her, one hand raking the gleaming chestnut waves back from his head as if he might tear it out.

'Look, Tristan, this was a mistake,' she said with an airiness she didn't feel. 'But it's done now so there's no point moaning about it.'

He stopped pacing. 'And if you're pregnant?'

She turned from her study of an ancient Japanese wall hanging and wet her lips. 'I'll let you know.'

He placed his hands on his hips and she tried really hard not to stare at his muscular torso.

'Look, if it's all the same to you,' she continued

casting around the floor for her discarded underwear, 'I could do without a post-mortem.'

She didn't look at his face but she heard his sharp inhalation.

'It's next to the cabinet,' he bit out, and Lily followed his line of vision to where her tiny nude-coloured thong lay crumpled in a corner. She marched over and snatched it up, balling it into her fist. No way was she going to inspect the state of it while he stood there towering over her like some Machiavellian warlord.

'Well, I'm going to bed,' she stated boldly, turning towards the back staircase and heading for the relative safety of her room.

He snagged her arm as she moved past him. 'Did I hurt you?' His voice low and rough, as if the concept was anathema to him.

Lily cleared her throat. 'Uh, no. It was... I'm fine.'

CHAPTER TEN

FINE.

She had been going to say *it* was fine, Tristan thought moodily the next morning as he stared out of his kitchen window at the grey London skyline. The colour reflected his dismal mood perfectly.

But last night hadn't been fine. It had been amazing, sensational, mind-blowing. The most intensely involved sexual experience of his life, in fact. And he hated that. Hated that he hadn't had the wherewithal to go slow, and hated that he hadn't been able to take her into his arms afterwards and carry her up to his bed. Make love to her again. Slowly this time. More carefully…

He released a pent-up breath and scrubbed his hand over his face, remembering how she had looked afterwards. Gloriously dishevelled. Her dress creased, her hair half up and half down where his hands had mussed it, her lips swollen from his kisses.

He could recall with bruising clarity the moment her body had sheathed his, her shocked stillness. And she had bitten him—marked him—because even though she had denied it he *had* hurt her. The thought made him feel sick. He should have been more gentle. *Would* have been if he'd known.

A virgin!

She had been a virgin, and afterwards he had been disgusted with himself for taking her with all the finesse of a rutting animal against a wall.

Damn.

If there had ever been a time he'd felt this badly he couldn't remember it. Maybe when he'd come across her in his father's study doing cocaine—or so he had thought at the time—with some loser she had just had sex with.

Correction: *hadn't* had sex with.

Damn.

His head was a mess, and last night, after the deed was done, he'd stood in front of her like some gauche schoolboy with no idea how to fix what had just happened. Which was a first. But what could he have said? *Hey, thanks. How about we use a bed next time?*

And what about her response? *Don't say anything,* she'd said, and, *I could do without a post-mortem.*

Damn.

He couldn't have been any more shocked by her off-handedness if she'd hit him over the head with a block of wood. On some level he knew it was a defence mechanism, but it was clear she also regretted what they'd done together and that had made him feel doubly guilty.

Not that it should. She was an adult and had wanted

it just as much. Things had just come to a natural head with two people available and finding themselves attracted to each other.

So he would have gone about things a little differently if he'd guessed the extent of her inexperience? If she'd told him! But that hadn't happened, and he didn't do regrets.

Tristan rubbed at a spot between his brows.

He might not do regret, but he owed her one hell of an apology for his condescending behaviour of the last two days. As well as his readiness to accept all the garbage that was written about her.

But hadn't it been easier to accept she was an outrageous attention-seeker like his mother so he didn't have to face how she made him feel?

Which was what, exactly?

Confused? Off-balance?

He took a swill of his coffee and grimaced as cold liquid pooled in his mouth.

He put his cup in the sink and stopped to look again at the morning papers on his kitchen table.

An earlier perusal of the headlines on the internet had confirmed that Lily's concerns the previous night had been well founded. A photo of their kiss was plastered over every two-bit tabloid and interested blog in the Western world.

On top of that someone had snapped their photo at the airport right before he had put her in the back of his limousine that first day. She'd had her hand on his chest and the caption in that particular paper had read 'Lord Garrett picks up something Wild at Heathrow'.

Cute.

So what to do about her? Try and play it cool? Pretend he wasn't still burning up for her? And *why* was he? Once was often more than enough with a woman, because for him sex was just sex no matter which way you spun it.

But it hadn't felt like just sex with Lily, and that was one more reason to stay away from her.

The thought that this was more than just an attraction chilled him. He didn't do love either.

Damn. Who'd mentioned anything about love?

He blew out a breath and snatched the papers off the bench. One good deed. That was all he'd tried to do. And now his life was more complicated than a world-class Sudoku.

When Lily woke that morning she remembered everything that had happened the night before in minute detail. Every single thing. Every touch, every kiss, the scent of him, the feel of him...

She rolled onto her back and stared at the crystal chandelier above her bed. She loved that these perfect antiques were woven into the ultra-modern décor of his amazing home.

Part of her wanted to regret last night. The part that had been hurt by his obvious rejection straight afterwards. But another part told her to get over it. She'd had sex. Big deal. People did it every day. Granted, it probably wasn't the smartest thing to have sex with a playboy type who thought she belonged in a sewer… but at least she hadn't made her mother's grave error and fallen in love with him.

And in a way it had been necessary. Tristan had been right when he'd said there was unfinished business between them. As much as she'd tried to deny it there had been, and now it was gone. Finished—as it were.

It wasn't as if Tristan had promised her a happy-ever-after. And even if he had she didn't want one. So what was there to regret? Except having to face him again. That could be awkward. Oh, and the small matter of an unplanned pregnancy. She didn't know how that had slipped her mind. Not that she was worried. She trusted the universe too much to believe that was a possibility, and she was still in the early part of her cycle so that was safe—wasn't it? She'd never had to consider it before, and those sketchy high school lessons on the birds and bees weren't holding up very well ten years down the track.

Pushing aside her thoughts, she glanced around the elegant, tastefully decorated room. His whole house was like that. State-of-the-art and hideously expensive. Lots of wide open spaces, acres of polished surfaces, toe-curlingly soft carpets against contrasting art and antiquities. And it was neat. Super neat. But that was most likely his housekeeper's doing, because his office was another story altogether.

It made her wonder at the person he was. Because

as much as she wanted to hate him she knew she didn't. Most of his actions, she knew, were driven by a deep-seated sense of responsibility and a desire to look out for his sister, and even though he had been harsh with her he'd also been incredibly tender. If she was being completely honest with herself, his sharp intellect and take-no-prisoners attitude had always excited her.

Lily felt herself soften, and swung her legs onto the boldly striped Tai Ping carpet and headed for the shower, her body tender from his powerful lovemaking.

She showered quickly and smoothed rosehip oil all over her face and arms, running a critical eye over herself. She knew her face was much lauded, but like anyone she had her problems. A tendency for her skin to look sallow, and dark circles that materialised under her eyes as soon as she even thought about not getting eight hours sleep a night. Right now they looked like bottomless craters, and she reached for her magic concealer pen to hide the damage of another night with very little sleep.

Discarding the towel she had wrapped around her body, she donned her silk robe and felt the flow of the fabric across her sensitised skin. Her breasts firmed and peaked, and just like that she was back in Tristan's living room with his mouth sweetly tugging on her flesh.

Stop thinking about it, she berated herself. She was an intelligent woman who paid her own bills and made her own bed, and yet the only bed she could think of at the minute was Tristan's—with both of them in it! And since he wasn't thinking the same thing why torture herself with fantasies? She should be thinking about how she was going to face him still feeling so...so aroused!

A knock on the outer door brought her head around and she turned sharply towards the bedroom. It would be Tristan because she knew it was still too early for his housekeeper to have arrived, and she berated herself for dithering in front of the mirror for so long. It would have been more prudent to meet him downstairs, fully clothed.

'Come in,' she called reluctantly, tightening the sash around her robe and crossing her arms over her chest.

He did. And he looked gorgeous and refreshed. Just how she wanted to feel.

He walked over and dropped a couple of newspapers on her bed, and then stood regarding her, his hands buried in his pockets. His hair, still damp, curled enticingly around the nape of his neck and his olive skin gleamed darkly against his pale blue shirt. But it was his guarded expression that eventually held her attention. A level of awkwardness about his stance that gave her pause.

'I owe you an apology.'

'For last night?' Her voice was sharp and she moistened her lips. 'That's not necessary.'

'Yes, it is.' His voice was that of a polite stranger.

'If I had known it was your first time I never would have let things go so far.'

Lily sighed. She had been trying not to feel bad about what had happened last night but his open regret wasn't helping. Nor was the way he paced back and forth. 'I think we should just forget it ever happened,' she said, not quite able to meet his eyes. Lord, was this worse than his rejection of her six years ago? 'As you already said, we had unfinished business—and now…now we don't.'

He stopped pacing. 'And you're okay with that?'

'Of course. Aren't you?'

'Of course.'

Lily nodded. Of course. What had she expected? A declaration of love? Even the thought was ludicrous, because she absolutely didn't want that.

'So…'

'I also want to apologise for my attitude towards you when I picked you up. For accusing you of using drugs and knowingly bringing them into the country,' he said.

Lily's eyebrows shot skyward. 'So because I was a virgin I'm innocent of drug smuggling as well? Gosh, if only I'd thought to tell the customs official it would have saved all this hassle.'

Tristan threw her a baleful look. 'Your virginity has nothing to do with my reasoning.'

'No?'

'No,' he said irritably. 'I had already worked out

you weren't a user before then. And you'll be pleased to know I've fired my investigator.'

'Shooting the messenger you mean?' she jeered.

'His work was substandard—even with the limited time frame he had to collate the information. Hell, I thought you'd be happy to hear that.'

'Happy that a man lost his job because he confirmed your view of me? He probably just gave you what you wanted, like everybody else does,' she said caustically.

'Don't push it, Lily. You weren't exactly forthcoming with the truth when I questioned you.'

'That's because I don't find it beneficial to bash my head against a brick wall.'

She saw a muscle tick in his jaw as he regarded her from under hooded eyes.

'Tell me why I found you hiding a joint under Jo's mattress when you were fourteen.'

'I thought you were apologizing?' she countered.

'I did.'

'It could use some work.'

Tristan said nothing, his expression coolly assessing. It was a look Lily had come to recognise. It meant that he fully intended to get his own way.

'Don't use your courtroom tactics with me, Tristan,' she said frostily. 'They won't work.'

'Would it help if I tell you Jordana has already admitted that it was hers?'

Lily tried to keep her surprise from showing. 'When?'

'The day of your apprehension at Heathrow. I didn't believe her at the time.'

Lily placed her hand against her chest with a flourish. 'Oh, and for a minute there I felt so special.'

She could see her sarcasm had irritated him, but he rubbed a hand across his eyes before piercing her with his gaze again.

'It's confession time, Lily. I know my sister hasn't been the saint I've wanted her to be, and I'm tired of the misunderstandings between us.'

Lily thought about arguing—but what was the point? He'd only get his own way in the end.

'If you remember, you visited our boarding school on a surprise birthday visit for Jo—only she saw you from the rec room. She called me on the internal phone and asked me to hide it. I hadn't expected you would walk in without knocking.'

'And the night of Jo's eighteenth? In my father's study? No evading the answer this time.'

'You should ask Jordana.'

'I'm asking *you*.'

Lily crossed the floor and sat on the striped Rein occasional chair in the corner. 'I don't know how the party in your dad's study got started. I was tipped off by a mutual friend, and by the time I got there it was in full swing. I felt responsible, because the guy who'd brought the drugs worked for my stepfather's company, but no one listened when I told them to clean it up. So I decided to step in and do it myself and—'

'I walked in, put two and two together, and came up with several hundred.'

'Something like that.'

'And you didn't think to defend yourself?' His tone was accusatory.

'You didn't exactly give me much of a chance, remember?' she felt stung into retorting.

Tristan shook his head and strode over to the window, pushing the heavy curtain aside to stare outside.

Lily shifted and tucked her legs under her on the chair, absently noting how the light from the incoming sun picked up the bronzed highlights in his hair.

Then he turned back, his expression guarded. 'I'm sorry.'

Did he *have* to look quite so good-looking?

She cleared her throat and shifted uncomfortably on her seat. If he was apologising why did she suddenly feel so nervous? 'It's fine; I shouldn't have invited that guy in the first place.'

He shrugged as if that were inconsequential. 'I shouldn't have jumped to conclusions. I...I wasn't quite myself that night.'

Lily's mind immediately spun back to the dance floor. The kiss. Had he not been himself then either? How embarrassing.

'Me either,' she lied.

He nodded, as if that solved everything, and Lily's heart sank a little. 'Was there something else?'

He shook his head and then glanced towards her bed.

'Actually, yes.' He pointed to the bed. 'I'm sorry to say that your premonition about the photos has come true.'

Lily rose and walked over to the bed. 'Oh.'

'I said a little more than that myself,' he acknowledged ruefully.

'I did too.' She glanced up briefly. 'Internally…'

She thought a momentary smile curved his mouth, but it might easily have been a trick of the light given how stiff and remote he seemed.

'I should go.'

'Yes,' Lily agreed, following him with her eyes as he walked to the door. Then he stopped abruptly.

'Are you…okay this morning?' His voice was rough and slightly aggressive and she knew what he was asking.

'I thought we'd just agreed to forget last night?'

'I'm allowed to check how you are, dammit. And don't say *fine*.'

She arched an eyebrow. 'Will great do?' she asked lightly.

His nostrils flared and she thought that maybe now was not a good time to aggravate him.

Tristan's mouth tightened. This situation was intolerable. He couldn't be in the same room with her and not want to touch her, but it was obvious by the proud tilt of her head that she wouldn't welcome his advances. He didn't know what he had expected from her this morning, but her suggestion that they forget last night had surprised him. And annoyed him. Because he wasn't sure he *could* forget it!

The phone in his pocket rang and he checked the caller ID before answering. Bert had been caught in a six-car pile-up on Rosslyn Hill. He didn't want another car. He'd call a cab—it would be quicker.

'What happened?'

'Bert's been caught in an accident.'

'Is he okay?' Her concern was genuine, and he was reminded of how yesterday she had given Bert unsolicited signed promotional pictures of herself when she found out his daughters were fans.

'It was minor, but he's wedged between two other cars. I'll arrange someone to help him out and call a cab.'

'I'll get dressed.'

Tristan's eyes drifted down over the dove-grey silk wrap she wore and he noted the delicate pink that swept into her face. Even with the shadows beneath her eyes she was quite simply the most beautiful woman he had ever seen.

'Good idea.'

Twenty minutes later Lily joined Tristan on a rear terrace that looked out over a sizable manicured garden flanked by a glassed-in pool and gymnasium, absently noting that it was hard to believe she was in the middle of one of the busiest cities in the world.

Tristan wore his suit jacket now, and she felt like a tourist in her simple jeans, white T-shirt and faithful black cardigan. She noticed him glance at her cardigan as he watched her approach, a bemused expression flitting across his face.

'What?'

'Nothing.' He shook his head. 'I would offer you tea, but I'd like to get going and check that Bert is okay.'

'Sure.' Lily followed him back through the house towards the front door.

'It seems traffic is particularly bad this morning. The cab driver has had to park up the road a way.'

'That's okay.' Lily smiled. 'I like walking. It's a New York pastime.'

'I suppose it is,' Tristan agreed, feeling awkward and out of sorts after her disclosures in her bedroom. His instincts warned him to keep his distance from her. After last night she was more dangerous to his emotional well-being than she had ever been, and in hindsight having sex with her had been a terrible idea.

Lily waited for him to open the front door and stepped out ahead of him—straight into the view of at least twenty members of the press, who had breached his security gates and were filling the normally pristine space of his forecourt, trampling grass and flowerbeds as they jostled for position.

They shouted an endless list of questions as camera flashes momentarily blinded them both.

It was like a scene from a bad movie, and after a

split second of shocked inertia Tristan grabbed Lily around the waist and hauled her back inside.

'Oh, my gosh!'

'I'll call the police,' he stated grimly, slamming the door shut before he turned to her and grabbed her chin between his thumb and forefinger. 'Are you okay?' His eyes scanned her face for signs of distress, wondering if perhaps she might have a panic attack.

'I'm fine,' she confirmed. 'I told you, I rarely have attacks any more—and, anyway, you grabbed me so quickly I barely had time to register they were even there.'

She smiled and he trailed a finger down her cheek, noting the way her eyes widened and darkened. Tristan felt his body harden and tamped down on the response. He was supposed to be forgetting last night and keeping his distance.

He dropped his hand and stalked through the house until he reached the kitchen.

'I'm sorry. I should have expected this…' she said.

Tristan shook his head. Not sure if he was more agitated at himself, her, or the hyenas filling his front garden. 'I don't know how you live like this.'

She swallowed. 'It's not normally this bad. In New York you get followed sometimes, but it's different here.'

'It's disgusting.'

'I'm sorry.'

He swore, and Lily flinched.

'Stop apologising. It's not your fault,' he bit out.

'If anything it's mine.' He raked a hand through his hair and pulled his mobile out of his pocket. 'Make a coffee, or something. We might be a while.'

'Do you want one?'

'No, thanks.'

After a brief interlude in his study, Tristan strode out into his rear garden and found Lily sipping tea on a stone bench, studying one of the statues that dotted his garden.

'Plans have changed,' he said brusquely, not enjoying the way she seemed to fit so seamlessly into his home.

'Oh?' Lily replied, confused.

'We leave for Hillesden Abbey in an hour.'

'How?'

'Helicopter.'

'Helicop…? But I have a dress fitting today with Jo.'

'You *had* a dress fitting. The seamstress will travel to the Abbey during the week to meet with you.'

'But surely Chanel don't…?'

'Yeah, they do. Now, stop arguing. A car will be pulling up in ten minutes to take us onto the Heath.'

'Helicopters leave from the Heath?'

'Not as a general rule.'

Ten minutes later two police motorcycles escorted a stretch limousine along Hampstead Lane and pulled up near Kenwood House, where a bright red helicopter was waiting. A few curious onlookers watched as they alighted from the car—but no paparazzi, Tristan was pleased to note.

'Are you okay to fly in one of these?' Tristan raised his voice above the whir of the rotors.

'I don't know,' Lily yelled back. 'I never have.'

He helped her secure the safety harness and stowed their overnight bags behind her seat.

'I'm co-piloting today, but let me know if you feel sick.'

'I'll be fine.' She smiled tentatively and he realised she probably would be. She was a survivor, and quick to adapt to the circumstances around her.

He handed her a set of headphones and took his seat beside the pilot, not wanting to think about how that was just one more thing to admire about her.

He was looking forward to going home. His father was away on business until Friday, when Jordana would arrive to commence her wedding activities, but Tristan always felt rejuvenated in the country. And most importantly of all, the Abbey was *huge*. It had two hundred and twenty rooms, which should be more than enough space to put some physical distance between himself and Lily and still remain within the constraints of the custody order. He felt sure that if he didn't have her underfoot the chemistry between them would abate. Normalise. She'd just be another pretty face in a cast of thousands.

His chest felt tight as the ground fell away, and he berated himself for not thinking of the Abbey sooner.

CHAPTER ELEVEN

LILY closed the last page of the play and stared vacantly into the open fire Thomas, the family butler, had lit for her earlier that night. The writer had captured a side of her parents she hadn't known about. He had focused on their struggles and their hunger for fame and what had driven it, rather than just the consequence of it.

The result was an aspect of their lives Lily knew about from her mother's diaries but which the press rarely focused on. It was an aspect that always caused Lily to regret who they had become. She had expected that reading the play would imbue her with a renewed sense of disgust at their wasted lives—and it had, sort of—but what she hadn't expected was that it would fill her with a sense of yearning for them still to be around. For a chance to get to know them.

A log split in the grate and Lily rose to her feet and prodded at it with the cast-iron poker. Then she turned and wandered over to the carved wooden bookcases that lined the Abbey's vast library.

She had been in Tristan's ancestral home—a palatial three-storey stone Palladian mansion set amidst eleven thousand acres of parkland resplendent with manicured gardens, a deer forest, a polo field and a lake with swans and other birdlife—for four days now.

She'd taken long walks every day, as she and Jordana had done as teens, petted the horses in the stables, helped Jamie the gardener tend the manicured roses along the canopied stone arbour, and caught up with Mrs Cole, the housekeeper, who looked as if she'd stepped straight out of a Jane Austen novel.

In fact the whole experience of wandering around on her own and not being bothered by the busyness of her everyday life was like stepping back into another era, and the only thing that would have made her stay here better was if she'd been able to see Tristan more than just at the evening meal, where he was always unfailingly polite, and nothing more. It was as if they were complete strangers.

For four days he had studiously locked himself away in his study and, from what Lily could tell, rarely ventured out.

Lily paused beside the antique chessboard that was always set up in the library and sank into one of the bottle-green club chairs worn from years of use.

At first she had thought Tristan had flown them to the Abbey to avoid the constant threat of paparazzi, but it had soon become depressingly apparent that he'd relocated them so that he could avoid *her* as well!

And she couldn't deny that hurt. After his apology

back in his London home she had thought maybe they could build a friendship, but clearly he didn't feel the same way. Clearly the chemistry he had felt for her had been laid to rest after just one time together. She only wished she felt the same way.

Unfortunately, consummating her desire for him that night had resurrected an inner sexuality only he seemed to bring out in her. And now that she had experienced the full force of his possession she craved it even more.

'Want a game?' a deep voice said softly from behind her chair, and Lily swung around to find Tristan regarding her from just inside the doorway. She'd been so deep in thought she hadn't heard him come in.

Her heart kicked against her ribs at the sight of him in black jeans and a pale green cashmere sweater the exact shade of his eyes. He looked casually elegant, while she was conscious that she had changed into old sweatpants and a top before coming downstairs to read.

'I… If you like,' Lily found herself answering, not sure that saying yes was the sanest answer, all things considered. The man hadn't said boo to her for four days and now he wanted to play chess…?

'Can I fix you a drink?'

'Sure,' she said, not sure that was the sanest idea either.

'I know you're not fond of Scotch, but my father has an excellent sherry.'

'Sure,' she parroted, ordering her brain to come online. Her body quickened as he walked slowly towards her, and she straightened the pawns on their squares to avoid having him see how pathetic she was.

'You start,' he offered.

Lily tilted her head. 'Is that because you're so sure you can win?'

He smiled a wolfish grin. 'Visitor's rules.'

'Oh.'

'But, yes, I'm sure I can win.' He flopped into a chair and chuckled at her sharp look.

He had no idea.

She regarded him with a poker face. 'Is that a challenge, Lord Garrett?'

'It certainly is, Miss Wild.'

'Then prepare to be defeated.' She smiled, knowing that she was actually a pretty good chess-player. It was one of the things she liked to do while sitting around waiting for scenes to be set up on location.

She leaned forward, her ponytail swinging over one shoulder, and rested her hands on her knees, concentrating on the chess instead of on him. Given his overriding confidence she guessed he'd be a master player—and she'd need all her wits about her.

'You're good,' Tristan complimented her an hour later, as she chewed on her lip and considered her next move.

So far he had countered every one of her attacks and she was fast running out of manoeuvres.

'Did you enjoy your swim this morning?' he asked, leaning back in his chair, his long legs sprawled out on either side of the low table.

His question made her glance at him sharply. 'How do you know I went swimming this morning?'

'I saw you.'

'But you weren't there.'

'Yes, I was.'

Something heavy curled between them and Lily cleared her throat. 'So why didn't you swim?'

'It's your move.'

Lily looked down at the board. Had he really been at the pool? And if so why hadn't he joined her? Mulling it over, she carefully moved her bishop across the board—and then watched as Tristan immediately confiscated it with his marauding rook.

'Oh!' Lily looked up to see a wicked glint in his eyes. 'Not fair! You were trying to distract me!'

'It worked.'

'That's cheating.'

'Not really. I did turn up for a swim.' His voice was low, deep, and an unexpected burst of warmth stole through her.

'Then I repeat: Why didn't you have one?' She lifted her chin challengingly, sure that he was just playing with her.

'Because I didn't trust myself to join you,' he said dulcetly.

Was he flirting with her?

Lily's heart raced and she quickly averted her eyes,

not sure she wanted an answer. Her stomach fluttered alarmingly and she looked at the chessboard without really seeing it.

'Aren't you going to ask me why?' he murmured.

Lily looked up and, seeing the competitive glint in his eyes, realised what he was doing. 'No,' she said a little crossly, 'because you're only trying to put me off my game.' And she *wasn't* going to be disappointed by that.

He laughed softly and the deep sound trickled through her like melted chocolate.

They played for a short time more, and finally Lily threw up her hands when he cornered her king.

'Okay, you win.' She smiled, not totally surprised at the outcome. After the swimming comment she'd lost all concentration.

She wondered if now wouldn't be a good time to go to bed. A cosy ambience seemed to have descended, and with the crackling fire behind them it would be all too easy to forget that he was here, with her, under duress.

Tristan tried to ignore the heat in his groin as his eyes automatically dropped to that lethal smile of hers, before sliding lower to the tempting swell of her pert breasts beneath the loose T-shirt. Did the woman even *own* a bra?

Oh yeah, he remembered. A pink one… He felt his body grow even harder at the image of her standing before him in matching delicate lace underwear. He loved the thought of her in matching underwear—not that she was wearing any at the moment…

He got up to top up his drink and give his hands something to do.

He'd been avoiding her all week, only seeing her at mealtimes, where she'd been so coolly remote they'd barely spoken to each other.

But he'd seen her. Watched her take long walks in the park, listened to her musical laugh as she'd helped Jamie choose which roses would be cut for the house in preparation for Jordana's wedding in two days' time.

Before, he'd been honest about not trusting himself to join her in the pool that morning, but he could see she hadn't believed him. Which was probably just as well.

Because distance had not done a damn thing to dampen the need he had to touch her, or just to be with her—which in some ways was scarier than the other.

Emotions he'd never had any trouble keeping at bay threatened to take him by the bit and make him forget all his good intentions to avoid relationships of any sort. She was dangerous, he knew it, but he couldn't deny he was drawn to her flame. Some primal desire was overriding his superficial instincts to keep away.

And now, against his better judgement, he returned to her side, holding the decanter of sherry in his hand. 'Here, let me pour you another drink.'

'No, I should…go to bed.'

The words hung between them but he ignored her hesitancy until she raised her near-empty glass.

'One more won't hurt.'

He replaced the stopper and sat the decanter beside his chair. He wasn't sure what he was doing; he only knew he didn't want her to go yet.

'Mmmm, this is nice,' she murmured, sipping at her glass.

He leaned back and studied her. She looked beautiful, with her hair in a messy ponytail, no make-up and her legs tucked up under her. The space between them crackled like the logs in the fireplace and he knew from the high colour on her cheeks that she felt it too. At this moment she had never seemed more beautiful to him. Or more nervous. He wondered whether she would bolt if he described the scene playing out in his mind.

'I've noticed you going for walks every day,' he said, in an attempt to distract himself.

'Oh, yes.' Lily's enthusiasm lit up her face. 'It's such a beautiful space here. You're so lucky to have it.'

'What do you like about it?' he asked, curious despite himself.

'It's rejuvenating, peaceful—and so quiet. And I love that your family has left the forest untouched.'

All the things *he* loved!

'They used to hunt there, that's why.'

'Oh, don't spoil it.' Her mouth made a moue of disappointment and he laughed.

'Never fear, Bambi is safe from this generation of Garretts.'

She smiled and the almost shy look she cast from under her lashes caught him in the solar plexus.

'That's nice.'

'That's only because I'm not here all that often,' he teased.

'I don't believe you. And you're spoiling it again,' she scolded, picking up on the falseness behind his words.

'Come over by the fire?' he murmured, mentally rolling his eyes at the stupidity of that suggestion.

But she did, and he poked at the fire while she found a comfortable position on the Persian rug.

'What was it like growing up in your world?' she asked, watching him carefully as he sat down opposite her, his drink dangled over one knee.

Tristan didn't like talking about himself as a general rule, but he'd invited her to sit by the fire and couldn't very well ignore her question.

'Privileged. Boring at times. Not that much different from any other life, I expect, apart from the opportunities that come with the title—although that also comes with a duty of care.'

'What do you mean?'

He glanced at her, and then back at the fire. 'I take the view that being born into the nobility is about being a custodian of history. All this is grand and awe-inspiring, but it's not mine and it never will be. I'm fortunate enough to look after it, yes, but this house is a part of something much bigger and it belongs to everyone, really.'

'Is that why you open your home to the public?'

'Partly. People are naturally curious about the country's history, and my ancestors have accumulated a lot of important artefacts that deserve to be viewed by more than just a privileged few. Especially if those privileged few don't understand the importance of what they have.'

'Do you mean people who don't care about their heritage?'

Her softly voiced question brought his attention back to her, and he wondered at the looseness of his tongue and the need he suddenly felt to unburden himself of the weight of the less salubrious aspects of his history. He suspected, given Lily's dislike of the press, that she wouldn't run off and disclose his secrets—and really they weren't all that secret anyway.

'My grandfather was a heavy drinker and gambler, and he ran the property into quite a severe state of disrepair. My father had to work two jobs for a while to try and rebuild it, and while he was off working my mother thought a good little money-earner might be to sell off some of my father's most prized heirlooms.' He couldn't stop the note of bitterness from creeping into his voice.

'Oh, how terrible!' Lily cried. 'She must have been so unhappy to try and reach out that way.'

Tristan cut her a hard glance. *'Reach out?'*

'Yes. My mother did terrible things to get my father's attention, and—'

'My mother wasn't trying to get my father's attention,' he bit out. 'She was trying to get more money to fund her lifestyle.'

Something she'd talked about endlessly.

'I'm sorry.' Lily touched his arm and then drew her hand back when he looked at her sharply. 'And was your father able to recover them? The heirlooms?'

'No.' His tone was brittle even to his own ears. 'But I did.'

Lily paused and then said softly. 'You don't like her very much, do you?'

Tristan put another log on the fire and ran an agitated hand through his hair, realising too late that he'd said too much. How should he respond to that? Tell her that he would probably have forgiven his mother anything if she'd shown him a modicum of genuine affection as he'd been growing up? But she had, hadn't she? Sometimes.

'My mother wasn't the most maternal creature in the world, and as I matured I lost a lot of respect for her.' He spied the bound folio next to the stone hearth and realised it was the play Lily had been carrying around with her. 'What are you reading?' he asked, reaching for it.

Lily made a scoffing noise. 'Not a very subtle conversation change, My Lord. And not a very good one either. It's a play about my parents.'

'The one that slimeball reporter asked you about?'

She shifted uncomfortably and he wondered about that.

'Yes.'

'But you don't want to do it?'

'No.'

He watched the way the firelight warmed her angelic features and wondered what was behind her reticence to do the play. 'Tell me about your life,' he surprised them both by saying.

She shook her head. '*Quid pro quo*, you mean.'

'Why do you call yourself Lily instead of Honey?' he queried, warming to the new topic but sensing her cool at the same time.

For a minute he didn't think she was going to answer and then she threw him one of those enigmatic smiles that told him she was avoiding something. 'My stepfather thought it would be a good idea for me to change it. You know—reinvent myself. Make a fresh start.' She laughed, as if it was funny, but the lightness in her tone was undermined by the sudden tautness of her shoulders.

'How old were you?'

'Seven.'

'Seven!'

'I was a bit traumatised at the time—wouldn't speak to anyone for six months after my parents died.

Plus my parents weren't the most conventional creatures, so it was a good idea, really.'

'Jordana said you were named after your mother?'

'Sort of. She was Swedish and her name was Hanna—Hanny. When she moved to England her accent made it sound like she was saying honey—so everyone called her that. I guess my parents liked the name. Which was why it was such a good idea when Frank suggested I change it. It set me free to become my own person.' She stopped, more colour highlighting her cheeks.

Tristan didn't agree. He knew of Frank Murphy. His office had handled a complaint against the man some years back, and he had a reputation for being an egotistical schmuck.

Tristan knew the story about how Hanny Forsberg had married him in a whirlwind romance and then returned to her one true love a week later. Only to die in said lover's arms that very night. Tristan couldn't imagine Frank Murphy taking her defection well, and wondered if he had taken his anger out on Lily.

'I'm not sure that would have been his only motivation,' he commented darkly, swilling the last of his Scotch and placing his empty glass behind him.

'What do you mean?'

'I mean Frank Murphy is a self-interested swine who would have been looking out for his own interests before yours.'

'Frank's not like that,' she defended.

'Come on, Lily. Frank Murphy is a user. Everyone

knows that. And the accolades he got from taking in Hanny's orphan were huge.'

'Maybe.'

Tristan hadn't missed the flash of pain in her eyes before she shifted position and moved closer to the fire, her hands outstretched towards the leaping flames. He wondered what was going through her mind and then shook his head.

'I've upset you.'

'No.'

'Yes. I didn't mean to imply that Frank didn't care for you. I'm sure he did.'

'No. He didn't. Not really.'

'Lily, it's a big responsibility to look after a child that's not your own. I'm sure—'

'There was no one else.'

'Sorry?'

'Nobody else wanted me.' She shrugged as if they were discussing nothing more important than the weather. 'When my parents died I had nowhere to go. I would have become a ward of the state if he hadn't stepped in.'

'What about your grandparents?'

'Johnny's had died and my mother's were old, and they'd disowned her after her first Page Three spread.'

'But Johnny had a brother, I recall.'

'Unfortunately he used to get more wasted than Johnny and looking after a seven-year-old was not high on his list of things to accomplish.'

'Your mother—'

'There was no one, okay? It's no big deal. I think I'll go to bed.'

'Wait!'

'For what?'

'You're upset,' he said gently.

Lily shivered as if a draught of cold air had caught her unawares, and for a minute she seemed lost.

'Did you know I found them?' She held her hands out to the fire again, as if seeking comfort. 'The police kept it quiet, to preserve my "delicate psychological state", but I found my parents' bodies. It was Sunday morning and they were supposed to make me blueberry pancakes and take me to the park. Johnny had promised it would be a family day. Instead I woke up and found my mother lying on the sofa with vomit pooled in her hair and my father slumped on the floor at her feet. It was like some sort of Greek tragedy. If my mother could have looked down on the scene she might have enjoyed the irony of finally having my father in such a supplicating pose.'

Lily gave a half laugh and for a minute he thought she had finished speaking, but then she continued.

'At first I tried to wake them, but even then I knew.' She shook her head at the pointlessness of such a gesture. 'There's something about the utter stillness of a dead body that even a small child can understand. I knew—I knew even though I didn't know what was wrong—I knew I would never see them again.'

She stared into the fire for a long moment and

Tristan thought it was lucky her parents weren't here right now or he'd kill them all over again. Then Lily gave an exaggerated shiver and smiled brightly at him.

'Gosh, I haven't thought of that for years.'

Something of the anxiety he felt must have shown in his face because she turned back to the fire and sipped at the sherry she had barely touched. She was obviously upset and embarrassed, and Tristan felt heaviness lodge in his chest. He'd had no idea she'd suffered such a huge trauma at such a young age.

As if sensing his overwhelming need to comfort her she shot him a quelling look he'd seen before, but his mind couldn't place.

'I'm fine now,' she dismissed, but Tristan could see it was an effort for her to force her wide, shining eyes to his. 'Completely over it.'

No, she wasn't. Any fool could see that, and he didn't like that she was trying to make light of it with him. 'No, you're not. I think you hide behind your parents' controversial personas—the controversial persona you've also cultivated with the press. Almost as if you use your past as a shield so people don't get to see the real you.'

Lily stiffened, shock etched on her features, and then Tristan remembered where he'd seen that haughty look before. Right after they'd had sex that first time.

CHAPTER TWELVE

LILY stared at Tristan and willed the ground to open up and devour one of them. She'd been having such a nice time and now he'd gone and ruined it.

'You don't know what you're talking about,' she whispered, placing her glass carefully on the hearth and willing the lump in her throat to subside. She stared at the inlaid stonework around the fireplace and realised she was about to cry. Cry! She never cried, and she wasn't about to start in Tristan's presence.

'Lily...'

Lily quickly scrambled to her feet, holding her hands out in front of her as Tristan made to do the same. 'I'm...'

The words wouldn't come and she turned to flee, making it only as far as the upholstered French settee before Tristan caught her.

'I can't let you leave like this.' He spoke gruffly, swinging her around to face him and Lily promptly burst into tears.

She tried to push him away but he was like an immovable force and she pounded his chest instead. 'Let me go. Let me—' A sob cut off her distressed plea and Tristan gathered her closer.

'Lily, I'm sorry. I really am an insensitive fool, and you were right the other day. I don't know anything.'

Rather than making her feel better that only made it worse and she buried her face in her hands, unable to hold back her tears any more.

'Shh, Lily, shh,' Tristan urged, holding her tighter. 'Let me soothe you,' he husked, his voice thick with emotion.

Lily tried to resist, but somehow all the events of the week converged and rendered her a sobbing mess, unable to put up any resistance when Tristan sank down onto the settee and pulled her into his lap.

He continued to stroke her even after her tears had abated and Lily rested against him, her mind spinning.

Tristan was wrong when he said she hid behind her public image. It was just easier to let people think what they wanted. They would anyway, and really she didn't care a jot what anyone thought.

But if that were true then why had she turned her back on the country she loved and set herself up in America, where people judged her more on her actions than on her past? Why had she always tried to do what Frank expected of her? And why had Tristan's rejection of her hurt so much six years ago?

Lily drew in a long, shuddering breath and then released it, her body slowly relaxing in Tristan's warm embrace. Try as she might she couldn't find valid reasons for her actions. Valid reasons for why she let the press write what they wanted about her. It was easy to say that no one would believe her if she corrected them. But why not?

An image of her mother, wretched and crying, came to mind, and Lily squeezed her eyes against the devastating image.

But then other images crowded in. Happier ones. Her mother singing to her and towelling her off after a bath. Her father putting her on his shoulders as they strolled through Borough Market eating falafels and brownies. Visiting her mother's photo shoots and putting on make-up with her in front of her dressing-table mirror. Curling up with her father while he played around with his guitar.

Lily gulped in air and her heart caught. More unprecedented memories of her parents stumbled through her mind and she felt breathless with surprise.

She felt Tristan's arms tighten around her, one of his hands stroking from the top of her head to the base of her spine as one might soothe an upset child. As her mother had once soothed her.

Her father's mantra came to mind, trying to rescue her. But for once it didn't work. Because Tristan was right. She *did* care what people thought about her.

Slowly she lifted her head and peered up at him. She knew she must look an absolute fright, and was shocked when Tristan pulled the sleeve of his expensive cashmere sweater over his hand and wiped her eyes and nose.

'That's gross,' she grumbled, ducking her head self-consciously.

She felt him shrug. 'That's all I had.'

He chuckled, and Lily smiled into the curve of his neck. Being in his arms gave her a sense of security she hadn't felt since before her parents had died, and although part of her, the self-preservation part, told her to pull away, that she had embarrassed herself enough, that she was better off handling this alone, she couldn't get her limbs to obey. He was just so big and warm, and his rich scent was extraordinarily comforting.

But none of this is real, she reminded herself glumly.

'You can let me up now,' she said quietly, pushing back from him as those disturbing thoughts stole through her mind.

When Tristan made no move to release her completely she looked up at him. 'I said you can let me go now,' she repeated, in case he hadn't heard her.

'I heard.' He nodded, but didn't move.

'I think...I think I should go to my room and be alone with my misery.'

'Now, I was always told that misery preferred company,' Tristan jested.

'Tristan, please...' Embarrassment was overriding pain and Lily couldn't smile at his teasing words.

'I can't do this. You were right. I *am* a coward. I…I need time alone to think.'

Tristan curled his arm around her shoulders, preventing her from pulling further away.

'Thinking is probably the worst thing you can do right now. And I never said you were a coward.' He feathered her ponytail through his fingers as if learning its silky texture. 'You're one of the bravest people I know. And you're loyal and warm and smart. You've faced false drug allegations with dignity and you have a generous spirit. It's why people are so drawn to you.'

'People are drawn to me because of the way I look and because of who my parents were,' she argued.

He tapped her on the end of her shiny nose and she squirmed. 'You're too young to be cynical. And you're more than the sum of your parts, Lily Wild.'

Lily felt more tears well up at his kind words and buried her face against his shoulder again. 'You're a nice person. How come you don't show that side of yourself more often?'

He tensed momentarily. 'I already told you I'm not nice,' he said, his voice gruff. 'I'm just saying all this to make you feel better.'

'Oh.' Lily laughed as she was meant to. But he didn't fool her. He *was* nice. Too nice.

She shifted off his lap so she was sitting beside him, wanting to tell him what was going through her mind even though she'd revealed more about herself tonight than she had to anyone else.

'You were right before,' she began haltingly. 'I *have* used my past as a type of shield.'

'That's perfectly understandable, given your experiences.'

Lily paused. 'Maybe. But it's also helped me avoid recognising things like...like the fact that for years I've been so ashamed of who my parents were and how they died that I hated them. And I've let their destructive love for each other cloud the way I relate to people. You see, my mother kept diaries for years. Basically she and Johnny would binge on each other and then he'd go off with his groupies and my mother would cry and rail and swear off him—until he came back and the whole cycle would start over again.'

Tristan was quiet, and Lily's fingers absently pleated the soft wool of his sweater as she leaned against him and soaked up his strength and sureness.

'That sounds like the problem was less about how they felt about each other and more about how they felt about themselves.'

'What do you mean?' she queried, leaning back a little to look up at him, her eyes drinking in the patrician beauty of his face in the soft light.

He shrugged. 'I'm guessing Johnny Wild loved himself a little too much and your mother didn't love herself nearly enough.'

Lily digested his words and then blew out a noisy breath. 'Of course. Why did I never see that?'

'Too close to the trees, perhaps?'

She shook her head. 'You're really smart—you know that?'

No, if he was smart he'd get up and go to bed right now, instead of wondering what she would do if he reached up and released her silky mass of hair from the confines of her hair tie. If he was smart he'd be questioning this need to comfort her and touch her rather than just going along with it as if he had a right to do those things.

'Not always,' he acknowledged, feeling the air between them thicken as he tried to ignore her soft hands on his chest. 'You need to stop doing that.'

He heard the hitch in her breathing at his growled words and the sound sent a jolt of lust to his already hardened groin.

'Or…?'

He clenched his teeth against the invitation apparent in that one tiny word. 'There is no "or".'

'Why not?'

'Lily, your emotions are running high.'

She looked him square in the eye, her purple gaze luminous despite her reddened eyelids. 'And yours aren't running at all?'

He needed her to stop looking at him as if he was better than he was. 'That's not emotion, sweetheart— that's sex. And the two should never be confused.'

'Believe me, I know that.' She expelled a shaky breath but didn't remove her hand. Instead she slid it further up his chest and ran the tip of her finger underneath the crew neck of his sweater, along his clavicle.

'Lily—'

'I want to make love with you.'

Tristan wanted that too—but could he risk it?

She'd noticed his hesitation and her eyes had clouded over.

'Sorry. I— Look, if you don't want to I'll understand…'

'Don't want to!' His hands felt unsteady as they automatically reached out to stop her from getting up. 'Lily, you drive me crazy.'

She shot him a surprised look and he nearly laughed. Didn't she know the effect she had on him? Didn't she *know* why he had stayed away from her for four days? Why he should have stayed away tonight as well…?

'I do?'

'Oh, yeah.' His hot gaze swept down over her tear-smudged face, baggy T-shirt and worn sweatpants. 'Stir crazy…' he whispered.

He felt her tentative hands creep into his hair, and groaned when she leaned in and placed her soft, full mouth against his own. Oh, God, this was heaven—and he couldn't fight both of them.

He cupped her face briefly, deepening the kiss and sealing his mouth to hers. He flipped her over on the settee and shoved his hands under her T-shirt. She moaned and arched into his hands, and Tristan felt like a starving man being offered a king's dinner. He yanked her T-shirt up and fastened his lips on one pert breast, tugging at her sweet flesh, licking, sucking, drowning in the aroused perfume of her body.

'Tristan!'

Her loud gasp and uncontrolled writhing fed his urgent need, and he attacked her sweatpants and panties and drew them down her legs, frustrated when they became tangled.

He sat up and pulled them all the way off, and then knelt on the floor in front of her, not even caring that the floorboards were hard on his knees. He parted her thighs so that he could feast on her in a way that had kept him hard for more nights than he cared to count, but he stopped when he felt her stiffen.

'Tristan…'

Her voice was uncertain, and he remembered that she had been a virgin until a few nights ago and that maybe no one had ever done this for her before.

His hands instantly gentled on her inner thighs, and his fingers massaged her silken skin until he felt her muscles lose their rigidity.

'Take down your hair,' he whispered softly, gazing at her breasts rising beneath her T-shirt with her movement. A soft cloud of pure gold swirled around her shoulders and he inhaled deeply. 'Now the T-shirt.'

His thumbs kept stroking her inner thighs, slowly drawing them further apart, and he could feel tiny shivers of anticipation running along the surface of her skin. His own skin felt hot and tight, and it got even worse when she swept the grey T-shirt up over her head. Her breasts were standing proudly for his inspection, her nipples hardening into tight pink buds. Saliva pooled in his mouth at the thought of reaching up and capturing one, but he had other endeavours on his mind.

He glanced down at the soft nest of golden curls at the apex of her body, and then back up to her face.

'Let me,' he husked, desire beating like a fever in his blood. 'I've wanted you like this for ever.'

She wet her lips and arched involuntarily as his sure fingers moved higher up her softened thighs, bringing her closer to the edge of the settee as he delved between her damp curls.

She was slick and ready, and Tristan lowered his head and devoured her with his lips, his tongue, his fingers. She made the sexiest noises he'd ever heard, and when she came he thought he might too, lapping at her until he had fully sated himself with her taste. Then he rose, and felt like an emperor as he looked down upon her pliant flushed nudity.

His heart lurched, and desperation and need grabbed him by the throat as he quickly divested himself of his clothing and rolled a condom over his now painful erection.

She sat up and reached for him, but Tristan shook his head. He'd wanted to take things slowly this time, and already slow had gone the way of the birds. If she touched him he doubted he'd even make it inside her body.

'Next time,' he promised hoarsely, picking her up and carrying her back in front of the fire. 'I need to be inside you now.'

'Oh, yes.' She held her hands out to him, and Tristan settled over her and drove deeply inside her body on one long, powerful thrust. Her body accepted him more easily this time, but still she was tight and he tried to give her a minute to adjust.

Only she didn't want that and immediately wrapped her legs around his hips. 'More,' she pleaded, trying to move under him.

Tristan couldn't resist the urgent request and drove into her over and over, while he brought them both to a shattering climax that took him to the stars and beyond.

CHAPTER THIRTEEN

'I'LL be back,' he murmured against her mouth, and Lily flopped back against her pillows as Tristan quietly closed the bedroom door behind him.

She'd almost felt sick earlier, when she'd woken in the early-morning light to find Tristan trying to slip out of her bed without waking her. He'd pulled on his jeans, a frown marring his perfect features, and then he'd noticed her watching him. He'd looked remote, but then his eyes had devoured her and he'd walked over and let his lips follow suit.

'I'm going to make you a cup of tea,' he'd whispered, and she'd smiled and trailed her hand down his naked chest.

She didn't really want tea, just him, but she was glad now of the momentary reprieve as she stared at the ceiling and memories of last night swept blissfully into her consciousness.

Last night he'd told her she drove him crazy, and a slow grin spread across her face as she recalled the tortured way he had gasped her name when he climaxed. She liked the idea of driving him crazy. She liked it a lot. Because she felt the same way. She only had to think of him walking into a room for her hormones to sit up and beg.

Last night he had made love to her in front of the open fire and afterwards carried her to bed, where she had promptly curled against him and fallen into the deepest sleep she'd had since arriving back in the country.

He'd promised her slow, but she had no complaints about their lovemaking. In fact she'd loved it! The urgency, the excitement…the way he'd touched her, cared for her. In fact she loved everything about him.

Lily put her fingers over her face.

She loved him.

Oh, Lord. Did she?

She tested the words out silently in her head. And her heart swelled to bursting.

No. She couldn't. But she did. Completely and utterly.

And it had been there all along. It was the reason she'd been so nervous about seeing him again. It was the reason she had been so upset when he'd thought she was guilty of carrying drugs into Heathrow. That he'd thought her guilty of being a drug addict.

It was the reason she had been so morose these last few days, and the reason she had allowed herself to be swept away in the library last night. No, had *wanted* to be swept away—by him.

Lily swallowed, her heart pounding. They had

made love so reverently, and she had given everything to him and he had seemed to do the same back.

He'd told her she drove him crazy with desire, and although he hadn't said he loved her she couldn't believe he didn't have any feelings for her.

But even if he did what did that mean?

Nothing. Because he didn't do love. He'd made that clear enough. And he wouldn't want her to love him either. Only…what if he felt differently with *her*?

Right. And how many other women haven't wanted that to be true?

Oh, Lord, she was starting to go back and forth like an entry in her mother's diary. He loves me. He loves me not.

The man had just spent four days avoiding her—he was hardly likely to go down on bended knee after one night in bed with her.

Something she couldn't deny that she now wanted. Lily blew out a breath.

In admitting that she had fallen in love with Tristan it was as if a wall against all her secret hopes and dreams had come down. She wanted what Jo and Oliver had. She wanted somewhere to belong, someone to love her. She wanted something lasting.

She groaned audibly and rolled onto her stomach and grabbed her pillow. What did she do now?

Seriously she didn't expect him to declare his undying love for her, but she couldn't stop herself from wanting that. Yearning for it. But he hadn't looked pleased to see her this morning, had he? No. He'd seemed distracted. Troubled. She'd dismissed it after his ferocious kiss, but…

Enough! She raised a big red stop sign in her head. She wouldn't do this. Play mental ping-pong over a man. The best thing to do would be to wait. Because really she had no idea how Tristan was feeling, and until she asked him she was just making up stories in her head. Lovely, sugar-coated romantic stories. But stories nonetheless.

Deciding to stop mooching around, she checked the bedside clock and was shocked to see that it was already nine-thirty. And, even worse, it was Friday. Jordana was due at the Abbey this morning to start all her pre-wedding pampering treatments, followed by lunch with a couple of girlfriends, and then a rehearsal dinner for close family and friends!

Maybe she should have a quick shower before Tristan got back? Or maybe she should go and find him and remind him that Jordana was due.

But then her phone rang and took the dilemma of what to do next out of her hands.

Pushing the tangled sheet aside, she jumped out of bed and reached for her tote bag beside the dressing table. Fumbling around inside, she finally located her mobile and quickly checked the caller ID. It was the detective working on her case.

Her case! Somehow she'd forgotten all about it with thoughts of Tristan swamping her mind.

'Good morning, Detective.'

'Miss Wild.' His polite, modulated tones echoed

down the line. 'I apologise for not delivering this news in person, but due to workload issues I'm unable to travel to Hillesden Abbey today, and Lord Garrett was adamant that we inform you of any breakthrough in your case as soon as it came to light.'

Lily swallowed, her palms sweaty around the silver phone. 'And…have you had a breakthrough?' she asked breathlessly.

'Not just a breakthrough, Miss Wild. We've solved the case. Or should I say Lord Garrett has solved the case.'

'Tristan?' Lily shook her head.

'Lord Garrett contacted us two days ago, after finding a discrepancy between the personnel records we initially received from the airline and the records that had been e-mailed to him.'

Lily plopped down on the velvet ottoman in front of the dressing table and stared at a baroque wall plaque. 'I don't understand.'

'One of the attendants who worked on your flight was not on the personnel list we were given, and was therefore not interviewed and fingerprinted. We were unaware of the last-minute replacement because the person who dealt with the staff-change had forgotten to send the information through to payroll. As we were given the original payroll records the replacement flight attendant did not appear on our list and was therefore not part of our initial investigation.'

He went on to explain that when Tristan had started

looking into the case he'd picked up on the discrepancy and immediately informed the police.

'But why did she do it?' Lily asked.

'The flight attendant was bringing a small amount of narcotics into the country to earn a few extra quid on the side. When she learned that sniffer dogs would be going through not only the passengers' belongings but also the flight crew's she panicked, and you were an easy target. She was aware of your parents' notoriety and hoped that would be enough to prevent her own capture.'

Lily remained silent, struggling to process the information. 'So what happens now?'

'You're free to go, Miss Wild.'

'And the custody order?'

'Will be repealed by the courts some time today.'

Lily thanked the detective and sat for a few moments, completely stunned.

She was free.

She clasped her phone to her chest, trying to make some sense of it all. The whole sordid mess seemed surreal, and what stood out for Lily now was how sorry she was that her parents were still mainly remembered for their drug-taking rather than their artistic talents. Previously she would have felt suffocated by that. Tainted by it. But after her conversation with Tristan last night she saw that her parents had been only human. They'd made mistakes, yes, and paid the ultimate price for those mistakes. But they had tried.

It didn't mean she had to agree with their lifestyle choices, but nor did it mean she had a right to condemn them either—as many had condemned her. Except the author of the play hadn't judged them. He'd written a funny, informative and ultimately tragic account of their lives in a beautiful and heartfelt manner. And if she were to play her mother it could be her gift to them. Her gift to herself.

Lily felt short of breath at the surge of emotion that swept through her body.

Tristan. She wanted to talk to him. Share this with him because she knew he would understand.

She was free! And he had believed in her. Had helped her.

Lily sprang off the ottoman and grabbed the first items of clothing she found on the floor.

She wanted to feel Tristan's arms around her as he held her to him while she told him her news. Or did he already know?

She didn't care. She wanted to drag him back upstairs and make love with him. Run her fingers over his morning stubble—run her hands over his chest and take him into her hands as he had stopped her from doing last night.

Her body quickened, clearly agreeing with the direction of her thoughts and—

What if he's been working on your case just so that he can be rid of you?

The ugly thought weaved through her mind like

an evil spell but she immediately pushed it aside. No stories any more. Just facing her fears head-on.

'I couldn't believe it when Mrs Cole told me you were in the kitchen making a cup of tea. And why are you only half-dressed at nine-thirty? You're usually up with the birds.'

Tristan turned at the sound of his sister's voice. He was half-naked because he'd needed to get out of Lily's bedroom fast and had forgotten his sweater.

'What are you doing here?' he asked, a little more harshly than he'd intended.

'I have a little thing called a wedding at the local manor house tomorrow. Remember?'

Tristan rubbed his belly. 'I meant in the kitchen.'

'You didn't respond to Oliver's text last night about meeting him at the polo field at half-eleven, so when Mrs Cole mentioned you were in here I thought I'd remind you. What *are* you doing in here?'

'Fixing tea. What does it look like?'

He glanced away from his sister's too interested gaze and willed the kettle to boil.

'Who for?'

'Didn't you say you had somewhere to be?'

Jordana tilted her head, her eyes narrowed. 'Why is your hair all over the place? And what's that mark on your shoul—? Oh, God.' She clapped her hand over her mouth in a melodramatic show. 'You've got someone stashed upstairs!'

Tristan followed Jordana's gaze to his right shoulder and saw the imprint of Lily's fingernails from their lovemaking last night.

He'd woken this morning to find her curved in his arms, his upper arm numb from where she had used it as a pillow all night and a boulder the size of Mount Kilimanjaro lodged in his chest. He'd never woken up having held a woman all night before. In fact he usually tried to find a plausible excuse not to wake up with one at all, and he didn't mind admitting that having Lily snuggled against him like a warm, sleepy kitten had scared the hell out of him.

As had the feeling of well-being he'd been unable to dislodge alongside the boulder. If he'd thought the first experience with her mind-blowing then last night had been indescribable. She'd been completely abandoned in his arms and he... Suffice it to say it had been the most complete, the most intimate experience he'd ever had with a woman—even more unsettling than making love to her five nights ago.

He'd tried to sneak out of bed, but she'd woken when he was halfway into his jeans. He'd turned when he heard the bedcovers rustling to find her leaning up on one elbow, the linen sheet clutched to her chest and her golden mane spilling over one shoulder.

Her soft smile had slipped when he'd hovered over the idea of just walking out, but he hadn't been able to. Not after all they'd shared last night. He wasn't that big a heel. So he'd kissed her. Devoured her. Sucked her tongue into his mouth and very nearly forgotten why he had to get away.

'So?' Jordana prompted, bringing his eyes back to hers.

'None of your business. And keep your voice down.' The kitchen staff weren't close, but still he didn't want them overhearing. He turned back to the boiled kettle and filled the teapot, wishing that he hadn't sent Mrs Cole off when she'd offered to make the tea for him.

'I'll find out. I mean, she has to come downstairs some time…'

Tristan scowled at her too happy face. He'd be glad when this damned wedding was over and his loved up sister would go back to normal. 'Leave it alone, Jo.'

'Why? She must be important. Someone special?'

He put the kettle back on the hob and ignored her.

'Maybe it's a guy?'

'Jordana!'

'Just joking, big brother. Jeez, Louise, where's your sense of humour?'

Tristan turned away and asked himself the same question. But her next inane remark sent him into panic mode.

'That's okay.' Jo leaned against the bench. 'I'll ask Lily. She'll know.'

Tristan banged a lone mug on the tray. No way would he be having tea in Lily's room with his sister on the warpath.

'You won't ask Lily anything. You'll keep your nose out of my private life.'

'Why so tetchy? I'm only teasing you.'

'I'm not in the mood.'

'Well, that's obvious. Where is Lily anyway?'

'In her room.'

'Really?' She raised her brows at him. 'How can you be so sure? And isn't that peppermint tea? Lily's favourite?'

'I said leave it alone, Jordana,' Tristan growled.

'Oh. My. God. It's *Lily*.' Both hands were clapped over Jordana's cheeks. 'You're sleeping with my best friend!'

'Jo—'

'I'm so excited. I told Oliver I thought there was something between the two of you at the restaurant. I knew it. This is great.'

'Jordana, it's not great.'

'It is. I think you love her. The way you were looking at her that night at dinner... I told Oliver I thought it was fated. Lily getting into trouble and you bailing her out. It was as if it was meant to be.'

Tristan recoiled as if she'd slapped him. He was *not* in love with Lily Wild.

'Jordana, you're a dreamer. If I did care for Lily Wild it would never be serious, so you can forget about taking your romantic fantasy to the next level.'

'Why?'

'Because I'm not ready to get married, and even if I was Lily is not one of *us*. Now, if you don't mind, I have to start my day.'

Jordana didn't move from where she'd stood in front of him. 'That's very snobbish of you.'

'You can look at it any way you want, but I have responsibilities to uphold—and if there's one thing I've learned from our parents it's that love fades. You might want to believe in for ever after but believe me that's the exception, not the rule. I have no intention of falling into Father's trap and marrying a woman who might or might not be looking for an entrance into our society. One who will run away when she finds out there's a lot more to the title of Duchess than champagne and shopping.'

'Lily's not like that,' Jordana protested.

Yeah, he knew that. But he needed to tell his sister something to get her off his back, and if he told her that what he felt for Lily scared the life out of him she'd want to wrap her arms around him and kiss him better.

Anyway, he enjoyed his freedom. He liked having sex with a variety of women and he liked his life the way it was. Didn't he?

Tristan shook away the disquieting question. 'I don't care. I don't need love and I don't love Lily Wild. She's special to you—not to me. Personally, I can't wait until this damn drug case is over and I can get on with my life again. And the sooner you get that through your head the happier I'll be. Here.' The tea tray clattered as he shoved it at Jordana's chest. 'Take this to her, will you? And tell her—tell her...' He shook his head. 'Tell her whatever you like.'

'Can I tell her I think you're afraid and letting the mistakes of our parents get in the way of your own happiness?' she asked softly.

Tristan cut her a withering glance and stalked out of the room.

His sister had always been a child with stars in her eyes. It was why he and his father had protected her so much after their mother had died. She was too dreamy and too easily led. He remembered how he and his father had thought Lily would lead her astray.

Only she hadn't. Lily had actually tried to protect her.

He gritted his teeth. Lily hadn't turned out to be at all what he had expected.

He marched out of the kitchen and took the stairs two at a time as he sought refuge in his own suite of rooms.

Lily wasn't trouble waiting to happen. She was beautiful inside and out. He should never have slept with her again last night. It had been hard enough getting her out of his head six years ago, after one innocent kiss, and he doubted he'd be able to get her out of his mind as quickly this time when she left the Abbey.

Left the Abbey? He braced his hands against the sink in his bathroom and stared at his dishevelled reflection, wondering why that thought filled him with dread.

Because he wasn't finished with her, that was why. And by the look in her eyes this morning she wasn't finished with him either. They had started something last night—nothing permanent, but something definitely worth pursuing for as long as it lasted.

Jo had just panicked him before. Made him think this was more than it really was. But Lily herself wasn't interested in relationships and for ever after. Hadn't she said as much at Élan the other night? So what was he so het-up about? He didn't have to end things so abruptly; he could just let them run their natural course.

Lily pressed herself back against the hallway wall as Tristan stormed out of the kitchen, her hands against her chest as if that would make her thin enough to be invisible.

But he didn't see her anyway. He was in too much of a rage.

She let her head gently fall back against the wall.

It wasn't a cliché that eavesdroppers rarely heard anything good about themselves, and Lily was still trying to register exactly what she *had* heard. Something about her not being special. Not being one of them. That he didn't love her and couldn't wait for her case to be over so he could get his life back.

Jordana had said something after that, but her softer tones hadn't carried quite so clearly.

Lily felt the methodical beat of her heart as her thoughts coalesced.

She supposed she now wasn't left in any doubt as

to how he had felt this morning. That frown had been real and the kiss he'd given her had not. What had it been, then? Pity?

Lily reeled sideways and then righted herself. She wished she could go back ten minutes and reverse her decision to come downstairs looking for him.

Or did she? Wasn't she better off knowing how he really felt? Better off knowing that if she'd jumped into his arms as she'd wanted to do she would have just embarrassed them both? Wasn't this part of facing her fears?

A shiver of misery snaked down her spine and she blinked to clear her vision. She heard a rattling sound from the kitchen, and then voices, and quickly turned to sprint up the staircase before Jordana headed out to deliver her tea.

She made it to her room unseen and leaned back against the door, her breathing laboured and her stomach churning. Tristan's angry words were parroting through her brain like a DVD on repeat mode. He didn't love her. Didn't want to love her and never would love her. And, worst of all, she wasn't good enough for him.

She blinked. The shower. She would jump in the shower so that Jordana didn't see how upset she was.

In all honesty she hadn't expected that Tristan would wake up in love with her, but did he seriously think she was interested in his *title*?

Right now she'd like to tell him where he could

stick it—only then she'd have to admit she'd over-heard his conversation with Jo and she couldn't go there. Not without breaking down altogether.

Like her mother used to do over Johnny. Her mother had always turned to alcohol when Johnny had turned to his groupies, and where once Lily had looked back in anger at her mother she now looked back in pity. Because finally she truly understood what it felt like to fall in love with a man who didn't love you in return.

Lily felt as if she had a claw stuck in her throat as she let the hot water beat down over her face. As much as she might understand her mother a little better now, she also realised that she truly wasn't anything like her. She was her own person, and she wouldn't cling to Tristan, or rant or beg. She'd hold her head up high, tell him it had been great, and walk away.

Oh, Lord. She sucked in a deep breath and felt tears form behind her eyes. She remembered the moment she'd found her parents had died, the moment her uncle had said he couldn't take her, the moment her mother's best friend said she couldn't take her, the moment Frank had sent her to boarding school be-cause she didn't want to appear on his TV show any more, and the moment six years ago when Tristan had sent her away.

But none of that had felt anywhere near as painful as hearing Tristan say he didn't love her, and it was only Jordana calling her name from the other room that prevented her from sliding to the floor and dissolving into a puddle of misery.

CHAPTER FOURTEEN

WHERE the hell was she?

Tristan scowled as he leaned against one of the ornate oak sideboards in the main drawing room, sipping an aperitif and talking with one of Oliver's cousins while awaiting the remaining guests for the rehearsal dinner.

A waiter discreetly circulated amongst those already present, and Tristan glanced through the open double doors to where a lavish dining setting, resplendent with antique crystalware, awaited twenty-four of Jordana and Oliver's close friends and family for the rehearsal dinner.

From what he could tell the room was empty of everyone other than waiting staff. Which meant that Lily wasn't down yet.

Tristan knew he should have been in a better mood, given that his baby sister was marrying one of his oldest friends the following day, but he wasn't. After his run in with Jordana this morning his day had gone from bad to worse.

He'd been off his game during polo from the start,

and then Oliver had informed him that Jordana's 'surprise' for Lily was to set her up with all three of his single cousins!

Tristan had left the field immediately after that and discreetly cornered Jordana, telling her in no uncertain terms to rearrange the evening's place settings so that Lily sat beside him. Only she'd floored him by telling him that Lily had already asked that the place settings remain as they were.

Then she'd apologised for her earlier behaviour. 'Lily set me straight this morning,' she'd said. 'She told me she was just taking my advice and "cutting loose" by having a harmless fling with you, and that it was now well and truly finished.' Which had been news to him. 'I was just a bit carried away by the excitement of my wedding. I'm truly sorry to have teased you the way I did.'

Tristan had reassured her it was fine, but really he hadn't heard much after 'harmless fling' and 'cutting loose'. His memories of last night certainly did not fit under either one of those banners! And as for things being finished…

Did that mean Lily actually *wanted* to be set up with one of Oliver's cousins? This mountain of a man he was currently attempting to converse with, perhaps? Tristan hoped not, because objectively speaking he was an attractive devil. If Lily went for brawny males—and she had certainly been admiring his own muscles last night—then Hamish Blackstone would be right up her alley.

He scoured the room again for Lily and tried to clear the scowl off his face. Where was she? Avoiding him?

He'd deliberately stayed away from her all day to give her a chance to do girlie stuff with Jordana, convincing himself that the last thing either woman wanted was a male hanging around. But really, if he was honest, he'd been upset to find Lily constantly in his thoughts, and after their unbelievable lovemaking last night he'd needed time to think.

And what he'd thought was that there was no way she was getting it on with one of Oliver's cousins this weekend. Or the next, for that matter, and… Where on earth *was* she?

He was just about to go in search of her when the hair stood up on the back of his neck and he knew she'd arrived.

He turned to see her poised to enter the room from the single side door leading in from the south corridor and his heart stopped. For maybe a minute.

Not enough time to kill him, but long enough that it had to beat triple time to oxygenate his brain again.

George Bernard Shaw was meant to have said, 'Beauty is all very well at first sight; but who ever looks at it when it has been in the house three days?' Tristan could safely answer that he did! If anything, as he looked at her standing in the doorway wearing a powder-blue Grecian-style gown that left her arms and décolletage bare, with her glorious hair upswept, he didn't think he'd ever seen a more divine creature.

And by the intake of breath of his drinking companion *he* hadn't either.

'That's Lily Wild,' Hamish Blackstone announced under his breath.

Tristan grunted and waited for Lily to make eye contact with him. But she didn't. Instead she stepped straight up to a group of women that included the bridesmaids and Oliver's mother, looking relaxed and composed and every inch the movie star that she was.

'She's taken,' he found himself telling Hamish.

'You're joshing me?' the Scot spluttered. 'Jordana said she was single. Who's the lucky guy? I'll deck him.'

Tristan looked him up and down and thought he just might with those tree trunk arms. 'Excuse me. I need to mingle.'

He needed to talk to her, that was what he needed to do, and he didn't care who knew it. She couldn't just ignore him after last night.

'Cutting loose' be damned!

Lily smiled politely and answered questions about acting and America and everything else in between.

When she had first walked into the drawing room she'd sensed Tristan's presence and deliberately hadn't looked for him. She didn't want to see him. She had her pride, and she'd decided earlier that she wasn't going to collapse as she had wanted to do in the shower. That had been shock, and she'd had all day to steel herself against seeing him again.

Maybe it wouldn't be so hard.

He hadn't tried to see her once throughout the day, and since Jordana had set up a mini-beauty salon upstairs in her wing of the house she hadn't had time to see him either. Not that she'd wanted to.

What she was secretly hoping was that he would be glad she was keeping her distance and not make a big deal of it. He might even be happy about it. The last thing a man like Tristan Garrett wanted was a woman to go all starry-eyed over him. Or, even worse, over his precious title!

Which reminded her of how Jordana had said that Tristan was to be partnered with Lady Amanda Sutton at the wedding. A woman Lily had met at lunch earlier that day, who was charming, titled, and completely enamoured of Jordana's brother. Something Tristan hadn't told her about last night while he'd been making love to *her*!

'What was that, dear?'

'Nothing.' Lily smiled pleasantly at Oliver's mother from behind her champagne flute.

Lily let her anger at Tristan's subterfuge course through her. Maybe it was illogical, and maybe even a little unfair seeing as how he wasn't actually dating Amanda Sutton but Lily didn't care. She didn't feel logical right now. Or fair. She felt hurt and stupid and…empty.

Tristan had been magnificent last night. Strong, gentle, masterful, funny—every woman's ideal man come to life. Only he wasn't…or at least he wasn't *her* ideal man. Not that her body seemed to be getting that message. Even now it yearned for her to turn, seek him out, as if he was truly hers to touch and talk with. To laugh with and...

Oh, stop mooning, Lily!

It was time to smile and behave like the perfect maid of honour during the evening's festivities, and to do that she'd clearly have to make sure that any interactions she had with Tristan were later rather than sooner.

Which, okay, wasn't exactly facing her fears head-on—but one step at a time. Come Sunday she'd fly home and lick her wounds. Regroup. Forget Tristan Garrett.

'Lady Grove, Sarah, Talia.' Tristan's deep voice resonated directly behind her. 'Do you mind if I borrow the maid of honour for a moment?'

'Of course not,' Lady Grove murmured. 'I'm sure you both have final touches to go over before tomorrow.'

'Absolutely.' Tristan smiled. 'Lily?'

Okay, so sooner was probably a good thing. It would mean she could relax for the rest of the night. Or not, she thought as she turned towards Tristan and saw him dressed in a black tuxedo.

Oh, Lord, but he was sublime. And he'd had his hair cut. The mid-length layers framed his masculine features to perfection.

Lily couldn't suppress a shiver of awareness as he took her arm and led her across the polished marble floor to a far corner of the room. Fixing a pleasant smile on her face, she subtly broke free of his hold.

At least this was one scenario she'd had time to plan for. *No tears, no tantrums*, she reminded herself. No matter how much she felt as if she was falling apart inside.

She lifted her glass to her lips and glanced around the room at the other guests, as if she didn't have a care in the world. But Tristan squared off in front of her, his broad shoulders effectively blocking her view and giving her nowhere else to look but directly at him.

'If you think you're sitting next to Hamish Blackstone tonight you've got another thing coming,' he ground out between clenched teeth.

Lily blinked, wide-eyed at his fervent tone. She had no idea what he was talking about.

Tristan knew he had surprised Lily with the dark vehemence in his voice. Hell, he'd shocked himself.

He'd known as soon as he'd laid eyes on her that she was miffed, and he planned to find out what was bothering her and fix it.

He'd thought maybe she was upset that he hadn't brought her tea up this morning. Or hadn't sought her out during the day. Both theories he'd have put money on, but now he knew she'd taken umbrage at his tone as well, and logically he couldn't blame her.

'Excuse me?' she said with icy disdain.

Yep, she was definitely annoyed with him.

'You heard.' No way was he backing down now. She had to know she wasn't sitting next to anyone but him tonight.

'But maybe *you* didn't,' she said stiffly. 'I'm no longer under your protective custody any more. You're free to get on with your own life. Get on with Lady Sutton.'

Tristan's eyes narrowed. 'What does Amanda have to do with this?'

'She's your guest at the wedding.'

Tristan shoved his hands in his pockets and relaxed back on his heels. She was jealous. Hell, he hadn't even come up with that one. He'd quite forgotten he'd agreed to partner Amanda at the wedding.

'She's no threat to you. She's just a family friend, and she isn't really my guest.'

Lily gave a derisive laugh. 'I'm not threatened.' She tilted her champagne flute towards the light and watched the bubbles fizz. 'But the local grapevine says she wants to be a lot *more* than just a family friend, and she does have the correct *lineage*.'

Tristan frowned. As if he cared about Amanda's lineage… 'Forget Amanda. She's irrelevant.'

'She'd no doubt be upset to hear you say that.'

Tristan frowned. This conversation was not going at all as he'd planned. He declined a glass of champagne as a passing waiter stopped, and determinedly turned his back on an Italian count he'd befriended at Harvard.

'I'd like to thank you for your help in solving my case,' she said politely.

'It was nothing.' Tristan waved away her gratitude.

'Still, I'd like to pay you for your services and—'

'*Pay* me!' Tristan thundered, halting her mid-sentence. 'Don't be absurd, Lily.'

She didn't seem pleased with his response, but no way was she paying him for something he'd wanted to do for her—had *needed* to do for her.

His narrowed eyes lingered on her face. 'Is this because I didn't bring you your tea this morning?'

'I beg your pardon?'

'Don't play games, Lily. You know what I'm talking about.'

She raked him with her gaze and he felt as if she'd actually touched him.

'Or are you upset because I didn't try to see you today?'

'Didn't you? I didn't notice.' She smiled, her wide kohl-rimmed eyes staring at him as if she'd like to slice him in half, her glossy peach-coloured lips clamped together tightly.

He wondered incongruously how the gloss tasted and felt an overpowering need to prise those lips apart and sweep his tongue inside the warm haven of her mouth. At least then they'd be communicating a little better than they were now.

'Look, I'm sorry. I would have but I thought you'd be— Damn, did I mark you?' His eyes had drifted down over her neck to where a slight shadow marred her golden skin.

'Er...no.' She automatically lifted her hand to the exact spot he had been talking about. 'I...scratched myself with the hairbrush.'

He didn't even try to curb the grin that spread across his face. *Hairbrush, my foot.*

'What's wrong?' he murmured softly, deciding it was time to cut to the chase.

She shrugged and glanced over his shoulder at the nearby guests. 'Wrong? What could be wrong?'

'I don't know. That's why I'm asking. But I'm not going to keep at it all night.'

That brought her eyes back to his. 'Is that supposed to be a threat?'

Why couldn't she just be happy he was willing to ask about her feelings? He knew plenty of his friends who wouldn't have been. Hell, *he* would never have even considered having this type of conversation before Lily. He would have moved on long ago.

So what's different this time?

He couldn't answer his own question and so pushed it aside.

He ran a hand through his hair and shifted the weight on his feet. 'Lily, we had wild, uninhibited sex last night and now you can barely look at me. What's wrong?'

She smoothed at an invisible smudge on her cheek. 'I hardly think this is the place for that type of discussion.'

Tristan let out a frustrated breath. 'I couldn't agree more.' He grabbed hold of her elbow and all but frog-marched her across the room, smiling pleasantly at the familiar faces milling around but avoiding all eye contact.

He reached the side door and drew Lily out into the family's private corridor. She hadn't made a fuss, but then he'd been counting on the fact that she wouldn't.

He stopped beside a spindly hall table that was probably a thousand years old and turned, hands on hips, legs apart. 'Now talk.'

Lily folded her arms across her chest. 'Is this your usual approach after a night with a woman?'

'Don't push me, Lily.'

'Ah—your favourite expression comes out to say hello.'

Tristan's patience was wearing thin, and he knew she knew it. 'What. Is. Wrong?'

'What's wrong? You're behaving like an ape is what's wrong. We had sex. What do you want—a reference?'

'It wasn't just sex,' he denied.

'What was it, then?'

'Great sex.' He smiled—a slow, sensual smile that was meant to cajole her out of her mood. Unfortunately it backfired.

'Oh, well, pardon me. We had *great* sex. What more do you want? It's not like it was anything *special*, was it? I thought you'd be pleased to be able to get on with your life and...' Her voice trailed off and she clamped her lips closed, as if she didn't want to reveal too much of herself or her intentions.

'And what? Now you want to play the field? Get every other man's attention?' That had been his mother's area of expertise. 'You want to get it on with one of Oliver's cousins now that I've broken you in?'

Her shocked gasp reverberated off the vaulted ceiling and he knew his comment had been a low blow. But, dammit, he'd wanted to hear her deny any interest in other men. And now he wished she'd slap him. Anything was better than being stared down by this icy creature who just wanted to get away from him.

'I'm going back in.' She moved towards the door and his hand shot out to stop her.

Something wasn't right. She wasn't anything like his mother and he knew that.

'I'm sorry. That was uncalled for.' His gaze fastened on her face and she stared back at him, her eyes glittering with barely veiled pain.

Then the way she'd spat the word *special* at him, and *get on with your life* registered in the thinking part of his brain.

'You overheard me talking to Jordana this morning.' His tone was accusatory when he hadn't meant it to be, and her eyebrows hit her hairline.

'I wasn't going to embarrass you by mentioning it.'

'I'm not embarrassed.' Actually, he was still trying to recall exactly what he had said. He'd spent most of the day trying not to remember that particular conversation.

He tried to clear his head and think on his feet—something he was usually exceptionally good at, but which was eluding him tonight.

'You weren't meant to hear any of that.'

Lily shrugged as if it didn't matter. 'I'm sure you didn't say anything to Jordana that you wouldn't have said to me if I'd asked.'

Possibly. But hadn't he said he was sick of her case? And that she wasn't special? And something about his future title? Had he really said she was after that?

Okay, he could understand why she had her back up. He probably would have too if their situations had been reversed.

He shoved his hair from his forehead and smiled at her. 'I know you're not after my title.'

She looked at him as someone might regard a mutant rodent. 'What a relief.'

'And after last night you must *know* I think you're special.'

'How am I special?' she asked immediately.

How was she special? What kind of a question was that?

Tristan tugged at his shirt collar, annoyed when she held her hand up.

'Don't bother answering that. I think I know.' Her voice was full of scorn, and that got *his* back up.

Why the hell did he feel guilty all of a sudden?

They were both consenting adults, and she had asked *him* to make love to *her*!

'I didn't hear you complaining last night.'

'That's because I wasn't,' she agreed.

'Then what's the problem?' he asked aggressively.

'There *is* no problem. We had a good time and now it's over.'

'Just like that?'

'You want flowers?'

'Lily—'

She threw her hands up. 'Tristan, I can't do this.'

'Then how about we do this instead?' he murmured throatily, crowding her back against the hallway table, quickly reaching around her to snatch at a teetering vase that was probably two thousand years old.

He righted the vase, coiled his arm around Lily's waist and did what he'd wanted to do all day. Pulled her in close and sealed his lips to hers.

She resisted for maybe half a heartbeat, and then her mouth opened and his tongue swept inside. He groaned at the sheer heaven of her wildfire response and swept his hands down over the gauzy fabric of her dress. She gripped his shoulders and pressed her breasts into his chest. He wished he'd removed his jacket. And his shirt.

'Hmmm, nice gloss.' He licked his lips, tasting… cherries? And then nearly fell over the table himself when she let out a sharp cry and pushed him away from her.

'You *ever* kiss me against my will again and I'll slap you,' she said breathlessly.

'You wanted it,' he said definitely.

'No. *You* wanted it. I'm over it. And get that smug look off your face. Physically you're one heck of a package, but when it comes down to it you've got nothing I want.'

Tristan felt as if a bomb had just gone off in his head. His mind reeled, memories of his mother's words from over a decade ago dragging him under, but he shoved them away with steely determination, blanking the pain that threatened to tear him in half.

What was going on here? Was he actually about to beg? And for what? One more round in the ring? Not even his father had been that stupid. And Tristan could have any number of women. Didn't she know that?

He smiled—a true predator's smile. He'd nearly lost it over this woman and for what? Sex?

Forget it.

'Good to know,' he murmured evenly. 'Because unless you're willing to put out, *Honey Blossom*, you have nothing I want either.'

Lily's chin jerked up and she covered her mouth with the back of her hand and slowly wiped his kiss off before striding down the hallway. It was a good move. An admirable one. And he would have applauded her if she'd hung around.

Thank God he hadn't offered her anything more. Not that he'd been going to. He'd never offered a woman anything more than a good time between the sheets, or on some other serviceable surface, and Lily Wild was no exception.

He swore viciously. He hated her. God, how he hated her. Making him remember his mother, engaging his emotions like she had. Like some courtesan deliberately setting out to trap him. To make a fool of him.

He glanced down at the antique vase and nearly picked it up and hurled it down the long corridor.

He was happy she was gone because his instincts about her had been right all along: she was nothing but trouble.

CHAPTER FIFTEEN

TROUBLE with a capital *T*, Tristan reminded himself the following morning as he stood beside Oliver in morning suit and top hat at the entrance to the Gothic cathedral, making small talk with yet another expensively dressed wedding guest.

It was a splendid day—except the sun had come out to grace Jordana's big day and brought half the paparazzi in the Western world along with it. No doubt the combined news of Lily's near-arrest and subsequent release and the many royal attendants at Jordana's wedding was causing them to swarm like coachroaches. The local constabulary was also out in force, to keep intruders at bay, as well as a top London security firm that looked as if it employed some of the men from Lily's premiere.

And if Tristan was feeling slightly seedy—well, that was just the Scotch he'd consumed last night, after a dinner that would surely go down as the worst ever. Having to sit next to Amanda Sutton and feign a civility he didn't feel while Lily made eyes at one of the Blackstone boys hadn't exactly put him in the best mood.

'Smile, you great idiot,' Oliver grumbled into his ear. 'It's my wedding day.'

Tristan cut him a dark look and then gracefully bowed over some old dowager's gloved hand.

'And *why* is it, exactly?' he drawled.

'What?'

He waited for Oliver to agree on the splendid weather they were having with the dowager's daughter.

'Your wedding day?'

Oliver looked flummoxed. 'Is that a trick question?'

'You said you'd never give up your freedom for anyone.'

'That was before I fell for your sister.'

'You could have just lived with her.'

Oliver shook his head. 'And have someone steal her away at the first opportunity? I don't think so. Anyway, I want the world to know that she's mine. That we belong together. She's my soul mate, and I can't imagine a life without her in it.'

Tristan fidgeted with the wedding rings in his pocket. 'If that's not already a Hallmark card you could probably sell it to them for a few quid. Carlo!' Tristan shook hands with the Italian count he'd stayed up drinking with last night. 'Good to see you up in time for the ceremony.'

'You didn't tell me there was alcohol in that Scotch last night, Garrett.'

'Hundred-year-old.'

'That's the last of the wedding guests.' The wedding planner stopped in front of them and gave the Count a scathing once-over. 'So,' she spoke to Oliver and Tristan, 'if you'd both like to make your way down to the altar?'

Oliver led the way, and when they finally reached the front of the church straightened Tristan's tie.

'Leave my bloody tie alone.'

Oliver grinned. 'You could just tell her and get it over with,' he whispered.

Tristan scowled. 'Tell who what?'

The harpist started up, and Oliver dashed a hand across his forehead. 'Stop being a coward, Garrett. It's obvious you're in love with her. Just *tell* her.'

Tristan swallowed. Hard. 'Am I supposed to know who you're talking about?'

Oliver threw him a dour look. 'Unfortunately ignoring it or denying it doesn't make it go away. Believe me, I did try.'

Tristan scowled.

'Now, shut up and do your job, would you?' Oliver growled. 'And for God's sake smile—or your sister is likely to make us do this all over again.'

A look of utter joy swept over Oliver's face as he did the non-traditional thing of turning to watch his bride walk down the aisle, and Tristan swallowed heavily as he too turned, his vision immediately filled with Lily walking behind Jordana in a flowing coffee silk and tulle creation that curved around her sublime figure like whipped cream. All the other women decked out in their wedding finery, including Jordana in her delicate couture gown, couldn't hold a torch to his Lily. She was so refined, so poised, and yet so vibrantly alive—and then he knew.

Oliver was right. He loved her. Maybe he'd always loved her. The words slotted into his head like the final piece in a puzzle. Actually, the second to last piece of a puzzle. The final piece was how she felt about *him*…and by the way she avoided eye contact with him as she moved closer he could see that wasn't looking good.

Lily gazed around at the grand ballroom of the manor house Jordana had chosen for her wedding reception. It was filled with circular tables, each with an enormous central flower arrangement and ringed with white cloth-covered chairs tied with bows at the back.

Jordana and Oliver's wedding day had been picture-perfect and she'd never seen her friend happier. Jordana's beautiful face was still aglow as she chatted and smiled contentedly with her wedding guests.

'I wanted to thank you for being such a good friend to my daughter, Miss Wild.' The eleventh Duke of Greythorn surprised her as he stopped beside Lily's chair.

'Actually, Your Grace, it is I who feels blessed to have Jordana's friendship.' Lily smiled, completely thrown by the Duke's open warmth when previously, she knew, he hadn't approved of her at all.

'Tristan has informed me of all that you have done for Jordana over the years, and I know that if your parents were alive today they would be very proud of the person you have become.'

Lily felt tears prick behind her eyes, and if she'd been standing she would have dropped into a curtsey in front of this stately gentleman. He seemed to sense her overpowering emotions and patted her hand, telling her to enjoy her evening, and Lily watched slightly dumbstruck as he returned to his seat at the head of the table.

'Ladies and gentlemen.' The MC spoke over the top of the band members tuning their instruments and drew her attention away from the Duke. 'If I could please ask Earl and Countess Blackstone and their attendants Lord Tristan Garrett and Miss Lily Wild to take to the floor for the bridal waltz?'

The bridal waltz? Already?

Lily glanced around the room and noticed that Tristan had stopped conversing at a table in the opposite corner and was staring at her intently.

No way. She couldn't dance with him. She smiled serenely as she quickly threaded a path through the cluster of guests milling around on her pre-planned escape to the toilets.

She had managed to avoid being alone with Tristan the whole day, and had already decided that there was no way she could dance with him tonight without giving away just how brokenhearted she felt.

The band struck up a quintessential love song and Lily fairly flew out of the room—and right into Tristan's arms.

'Going somewhere?' he mocked.

Lily tried to steady her runaway heartbeat. 'The bathroom.'

'During the bridal waltz? I don't think so.'

'You can't dictate to me any more, remember?'

'No, but it's your last official obligation for the day, and I didn't take you for a shirker.'

Lily huffed out a breath and noticed the interested glances from the guests around them. 'I'll do it because it's expected,' she stated under her breath. 'Not because you challenged me.'

Tristan smiled. 'That's my girl.'

Lily was about to correct him and say that she wasn't his girl, but they were on the dance floor and he had already swept her into his arms.

She held herself so stiffly she felt like a mechanised doll, but there was nothing she could do about that. She couldn't relax, couldn't look at him. Then she remembered an old childhood trick she'd used to employ when she was in an uncomfortable situation. Counting. Once, she remembered, she'd counted so high she'd made it to seven hundred and thirty-five!

'You look exquisite today.' Tristan's eyes glittered down into hers and Lily quickly planted her gaze at a spot over his shoulder. One, two, three...

'But then you look exquisite all the time.'

Nine, ten...

He swirled her suddenly, and she frowned as she had to grip him tighter to stop herself from falling. He was wearing a new cologne tonight and the hint of spice was doing horrible things to her equilibrium. Nineteen, twenty...

'How's Hamish?'

Lily looked at him. She knew why he was asking that. She had found out from Jordana in a fit of giggles last night that her 'surprise' was to be set up with any of Oliver's three single cousins. Which was what Tristan had been so angrily referring to when they'd talked prior to dinner last night.

She hadn't known about Jordana's cunning plan then, and she knew Tristan's ego had been bruised when Jordana had fooled him into believing that Lily had welcomed her attempts at matchmaking. Which she hadn't. And she had apologised profusely to each of the men when she'd told them that actually she wasn't available.

They'd been completely charming, and she'd wished things were different so she might have been in a better position to invite their interest. But of course she wasn't. Her feelings for Tristan were too real and too raw for her to even attempt friendship with another man at this point.

Clearly Tristan's ego was still affected, if the way he was studying her was any indication.

'Fine, I expect,' she answered.

Tristan scowled and brought her hand in tightly against his chest. His other hand was spread wide against that sensitive spot in the small of her back. He was holding her so closely now Lily could hear the brush of her tulle skirt against his trousers.

Lily swallowed and concentrated on holding in the quiver that zipped up her spine, completely forgetting what number she was up to. *Damn.* One, two...

'Are you counting?' Tristan's deep voice was incredulous.

'Would you stop talking?' she whispered furiously, trying hard to ignore the growing tension in his big body.

Then he stopped dancing altogether, and Lily became acutely aware of the murmur of voices and the soft sway of Jordana's silk gown as she moved in time with the music. Lily stood in the circle of Tristan's arms, glancing around nervously at the interested faces of the wedding guests circling the dance floor.

She was just about to ask him what he was doing when he made a low sound in the back of his throat. 'Oh, to hell with it,' he muttered, deftly hoisting her and her close-fitted tulle skirts into his arms. 'Excuse us,' he threw at a surprised Oliver and Jordana as he strode past.

'What are you doing?' Lily squeaked, smiling tremulously as if nothing untoward was going on when it definitely was.

'Keep still,' he ordered, and Lily, not wishing to make any more of a scene, ducked her head into his neck just as she had done at the airport a little over a week ago, to hide her face from the amused glances of the wedding guests who were parting like the Red Sea to let Tristan through.

'Oh, I hate to imagine what everyone is going to think!' she fumed, scowling at the smiling waiter who had *kindly* held open the door to a smaller, private dining room and who was now in the process of closing it behind them.

She glared at Tristan, her heart beating a mile a minute, as he let her down, and stalked to the other side of the room, feeling marginally calmer with a two-metre-long mahogany dining table between them.

Tristan stood with his hands in his pockets and stared at her. 'They'll think I'm in love, I expect. Either that…' He paused as if to gauge her reaction. 'Or they'll think I've lost my mind.'

'Well, we both know the former isn't the truth,' she snapped. 'Don't play games with me, Tristan. I don't like them.'

Tristan blew out a breath. 'Lily, I need to talk to you, and this seemed the only way to achieve that objective.' He circled the table towards her, and stopped when he realised she was moving as well—but in the opposite direction. 'Would you stop that? I'm not going to bite you.'

Lily stared at him. He was so rakishly appealing with his ruffled hair and formal wedding attire it made her heart feel as if it was enclosed in a giant fist. She felt her old survival instincts rise up and did her best to blank out the pain of being so close to him and yet so far away.

'I'm getting a little tired of you thinking you can pick me up and carry me wherever you want. Next time it happens I won't be so concerned about creating a scene,' she warned with haughty disdain.

'Would you have come if I'd asked?'

His voice was soft, almost like a caress, and it confused her senses. Made her body soften. Lily did her best to clamp down on the rioting emotions running through her and focused on his question.

She lifted her chin and tried to stop her lips from trembling. Of course she wouldn't have come with him. She had nothing to say to him that wouldn't involve making a complete fool of herself.

'Say what you have to say so we can get out of here. I don't have much time left,' she added, thankful that her voice sounded steadier than she felt.

'Time left for what?'

Lily noted Tristan's sharp tone and decided now was not the time to tell him she was booked on the red-eye back to New York this very evening. After enduring the rehearsal dinner and feeling so tense a slight breeze might have snapped her in half she had changed her travel plans so she could head back to London and fly home to New York early.

Being around Tristan and watching him smoulder with Lady Sutton last night had nearly done her in. She loved him too much to imagine him with another woman, so seeing him with one who could offer him everything she couldn't was just unendurable. Better that she start her life again without him as soon as possible. Facing her fears head-on…or perhaps just running away. She didn't care which at this point. Her only criteria was that when she finally broke down she did so in private.

Lily steeled herself to look at him and lifted her gaze once more to his. He stood across the table from her, his expression as fierce as an angry warlord facing down a known enemy. She had no idea why. Had something happened earlier that she didn't know about and for which she was about to get the blame again?

'Are you going to answer my question?' he asked, almost too politely.

'Are you going to answer mine?' she parried.

Tristan exhaled and ran an agitated hand through his hair. He looked tired and strung out—very unlike his usually composed self.

'Lily this doesn't have to end.'

Lily, stared at him, not sure what he was referring to.

'*We* don't have to end,' he clarified, a strange, shadowed look settling on his face.

Lily wet her dry mouth. All she could think about was how last night he had confirmed that he really didn't want her. That she had just been an itch he had wanted to scratch. 'Last night you said…'

'Please forget what I said last night. I was hurt and angry.'

'Hurt?'

Tristan gripped the back of the upholstered dining chair in front of him. This conversation was not going at all the way he had hoped. Lily was supposed to have picked up on his lame declaration of love and thrown herself into his arms. Instead she was spitting at him and looking much the same way she had when she'd felt she had to defend her honour after they had made love that first time.

Okay, so maybe he wasn't going about this very well. But he'd never told a woman he loved her before. Had never *wanted* to love a woman before. Opening up about his emotions wasn't exactly his strong suit after years of holding them at bay.

He cleared his throat, more nervous now than he had been during his first courtroom appearance— which, come to think of it, he hadn't been nervous about at all…'Lily, I'd like to say something to you and if you still want to leave after that then I won't try and stop you.'

Lily stared at him, seemingly transfixed, as he walked slowly around the table and pulled out one of the dining chairs for her to sit down in.

She slid into it, almost with relief, and Tristan paced a short way away and then stopped, turning to face her.

'I told you the other night that my mother left my father, but what I haven't told you is that on the day she left, when I was fifteen, I overheard my parents arguing. During the argument my mother told my father she hated him and that he had nothing she wanted—that I also had nothing she wanted and that she was taking Jordana with her and not me.'

'Oh, Tristan.'

He held up his hand gently and shook his head. 'I'm not telling you this so you'll feel sorry for me. It has no doubt coloured my past relationships, as your parents have coloured yours, but I need you to understand something. My mother was not an easy woman to love but God knows I tried. There was a big age gap between myself and Jordana and for a while I was my mother's saviour. Her little hero. Then Jordana arrived, my father started working more, and I became relegated to the sidelines. I never understood why, and slowly, over the years, I learned to protect myself by switching my feelings off. I became angry with my mother and blamed myself. Two nights ago you inadvertently helped me see that what I hadn't understood was that my parents just had an unhappy marriage and I was one of the victims of that.'

'Parents often don't see the impact they have on their children when they aren't happy within themselves.' Lily offered softly.

'No.' Tristan shook his head. 'And it certainly put

me off wanting to risk my heart with another person, but…' He looked down at Lily's small hand enfolded in his, not even having realised that he had reached out to her. 'Lily, the other night I accused you of using your past as a shield, and I've only just come to realise that I do the same thing. I've put up barriers to my emotions my whole life because my mother's love was so unpredictable and my parents' relationship was so unstable and I don't want to do that any more. Actually, that's not completely true.' He looked up sheepishly. 'If I could still do that I probably would. But if I do I'll lose you, and after you walked away last night I realised that's more painful than everything else put together.'

Lily swallowed and looked down at their enclosed hands, then slowly back up to reconnect with his eyes. 'Why?'

Tristan leaned forward and kissed her. A kiss filled with all the love and tenderness he had been afraid to show her until now. He pulled back and waited for her eyes to flutter open. 'Because I love you, Lily. I think I always have.'

Lily shook her head, her expression dazed. 'You love me?'

'With all my heart. And the more I say it, the more I want to say it.'

'But you never approved of me…'

'Partly true. I disliked your lifestyle because I was always worried that Jordana would go the way my mother had, but really what I resented about you the most was how protective I felt towards you. Whenever I heard you were at one of your stepfather's parties, and I was in the country, I always came and got you out. I even did it once when Jordana wasn't with you. Remember?'

'I assumed you thought she *was* with me.'

'No. I knew she was home safe—and that's just where I wanted you to be. But it wasn't until Jo's eighteenth that my feelings for you changed. As soon as I saw you in that silver mini-dress I knew I couldn't deny that my feelings for you were more than just protective. I wanted you so much that night it hurt. But you were too young, and I was too closed to my emotions, and then when I came across that private party it was easy to blame you. It gave me an excuse to turn my back on the way you made me feel. But you changed me that night. I haven't been able to look at a woman since, be with a woman, without imagining she was you. Crazy, I know...'

'Not so crazy.' Lily reached up and almost reverently cupped his face. 'I fell so deeply in love with you that night I've compared every other man I've ever met to you and found him lacking.'

'Lily, does that mean what I think it means?'

Lily smiled and blinked back the tears blurring her vision. 'That I love you? Totally. Completely. How could you not know?'

Tristan felt such a deep surge of joy well up inside him he thought it would burst out. He grabbed Lily off the chair and hauled her onto his lap, crushed her mouth beneath his.

When he finally let her up for air he felt a sense of rightness with the world, but he could see by the way she gnawed her top lip that she still had questions.

'What is it?'

'I was just remembering yesterday morning, when you came out of the bathroom. You looked...you looked unhappy...and then you told Jordana—'

'Oh, Lily,' Tristan said on a groan. 'Please forget that. I woke up that morning with such a sense of well-being it scared the hell out of me. Honestly, I just wanted to get away from you. I've never woken up with a woman before and—'

'Never?'

He shook his head. 'Never. And then Jordana cornered me and guessed how I felt before I did and it drove me deeper into denial. I didn't want to let you in, Lily, but of course you were already there, and I was fighting a losing battle. It wasn't until Oliver told me how he felt about Jordana and the reasons he was marrying her that I finally realised I felt the same way about you. And I didn't want to fight it— you—any more. I'd do anything for you, Lily, and after we're married we'll—

'Married!'

'Of course married. Where did you think this was headed, sweetheart? A picnic in the park?'

'I...I didn't think that far ahead. I'm still reeling from the fact that you love me.'

'I know neither of us has had the best role models when it comes to marriage—'

'Well, my father never actually asked my mother to marry him,' Lily said.

Tristan nodded and cupped her face between his hands. 'I'm not your father, Lily. I'll never cheat on you or leave you. And I don't believe a marriage has to be full of conflict if a couple are equally committed and willing to work through any issues together.'

Lily's smile was tremulous. 'You really love me?'

'Haven't I just said that?'

'It just seems like a dream.'

'It's not. At least I hope it's not.'

Lily sighed and let Tristan gather her close, revelling in the feel of his hands moulding to her torso and fitting her against him. She could hardly believe this was happening, and knew Jordana would be ecstatic when she found out.

Then a thought struck, and she pulled back a little to look up into his beautiful face. 'You know I knew nothing about Jordana setting me up with Oliver's cousins last night?'

Tristan smiled. 'I know. I figured that out some time between the first and second bottle of Scotch I consumed last night.'

'Oh.' Lily laughed.

'It's not funny.' He grinned back at her. 'You were the reason I saw the bottom of both of those bottles.

But I have a feeling that my sister has been playing a little reverse matchmaking between us.'

'I did wonder about that myself...'

'And it worked. I nearly locked you in a tower last night after she said you'd told her you were just cutting loose with me.'

'I *did* say that.'

'What?' he asked, stunned.

'I didn't want her to know how deeply I had fallen for you and after overhearing how you felt. I...I have my pride, you know.'

'I know you do.'

'And, anyway, you don't have a tower.'

'I'd have built one for just that purpose,' he growled, his hands exploring the fitted bodice of her gown with increasing fervour.

'I love you,' Lily sighed.

'I never knew those three little words could sound so delicious.'

'Oh, I've just remembered. I'm supposed to be flying to New York tonight. I'll have to cancel the flight.'

'Damned straight. But when *do* you have to return to New York? For work?'

'I don't have any films lined up until next year. I was planning to take some time off.'

'Perfect.'

'Although...'

'Although?'

'I'm thinking of taking the role of my mother in that play I was telling you about.'

Tristan kissed her. 'I think that's a wonderful idea. You'll slay them. As you do me. Now, let's go upstairs.'

'Upstairs?'

'I organised a room.'

'But the Abbey is only two miles away.'

'That's two miles too far if I'm going to be able to make love to you with any level of skill and control.'

'I'm quite partial to what we've done so far,' Lily whispered, feathering the silky hair at his nape between her fingers.

'And I'm quite partial to you, my darling Honey Blossom Lily Wild.'

He bent to kiss her again but Lily dodged him. 'We have your sister's wedding to finish first.'

'Believe me, after the way we exited the dance floor nobody is expecting to see us back any time soon.'

'But I need to catch the bridal bouquet,' Lily protested as Tristan gathered her up in his arms and strode for the door.

'Why do you need a bouquet when you've got your groom right here?'

'I hadn't thought of that,' she admitted provocatively. 'Good thing you're here.'

Tristan stopped and caught her chin between his thumb and forefinger, raising her eyes to his. 'I'll always be here for you,' he said, capturing her lips in a sweet, searing kiss.

Lily's mouth trembled with emotion as she stared into Tristan's loving green gaze, happier than she had ever been in her whole life. 'And I you.'

* * * * *